"I don't want a perfect woman,"

Lucas said, moving closer to Jenny. "I just want her to be perfect for me."

Jenny stared at him, unable to say anything.

"I'm looking for a strong woman. Someone who won't crumble if the going gets rough. I want her to be able to stand up and tell me to go to hell if I'm wrong, or kiss me and tell me I'm wonderful if I'm right. And I want her to love and need children the same way I do."

Jenny didn't say anything and after a moment Lucas said, "You think I'm asking too much, Jenny? Or do you know a woman like that?"

Dear Reader,

Spring is on the way—and love is blooming in Silhouette Romance this month. To keep his little girl, FABULOUS FATHER Jace McCall needs a pretend bride—fast. Luckily he "proposes" to a woman who doesn't have to pretend to love him in Sandra Steffen's *A Father For Always*.

Favorite author Annette Broadrick continues her bestselling DAUGHTERS OF TEXAS miniseries with *Instant Mommy*, this month's BUNDLES OF JOY selection. Widowed dad Deke Crandall was an expert at raising cattle, but a greenhorn at raising his baby daughter. So when he asked Mollie O'Brien for her help, the marriage-shy rancher had no idea he'd soon be asking for her hand!

In *Wanted: Wife* by Stella Bagwell, handsome Lucas Lowrimore is all set to say "I do," but his number one candidate for a bride has very cold feet. Can he convince reluctant Jenny Prescott to walk those cold feet down the aisle?

Carla Cassidy starts off her new miniseries THE BAKER BROOD with *Deputy Daddy*. Carolyn Baker has to save her infant godchildren from their bachelor guardian, Beau Randolph. After all, what could he know about babies? But then she experienced some of his tender loving care....

And don't miss our other two wonderful books— *Almost Married* by Carol Grace and *The Groom Wore Blue Suede Shoes* by debut author Jessica Travis.

Happy Reading!

Melissa Senate,
Senior Editor

Please address questions and book requests to:
Silhouette Reader Service
U.S.: 3010 Walden Ave., P.O. Box 1325, Buffalo, NY 14269
Canadian: P.O. Box 609, Fort Erie, Ont. L2A 5X3

WANTED: WIFE

Stella Bagwell

Silhouette
ROMANCE™
Published by Silhouette Books
America's Publisher of Contemporary Romance

To my mother, Lucille,
for all the love and joy
she's given to me.

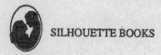 SILHOUETTE BOOKS

ISBN 0-373-19140-5

WANTED: WIFE

Copyright © 1996 by Stella Bagwell

Printed in U.S.A.

Books by Stella Bagwell

Silhouette Romance

Golden Glory #469
Moonlight Bandit #485
A Mist on the Mountain #510
Madeleine's Song #543
The Outsider #560
The New Kid in Town #587
Cactus Rose #621
Hillbilly Heart #634
Teach Me #657
The White Night #674
No Horsing Around #699
That Southern Touch #723
Gentle as a Lamb #748
A Practical Man #789
Precious Pretender #812
Done to Perfection #836
Rodeo Rider #878
*Their First Thanksgiving #903
*The Best Christmas Ever #909
*New Year's Baby #915
Hero in Disguise #954
Corporate Cowgirl #991
Daniel's Daddy #1020
A Cowboy for Christmas #1052
Daddy Lessons #1085
Wanted: Wife #1140

*Heartland Holidays Trilogy

STELLA BAGWELL

lives with her husband and son in southeastern Oklahoma, where she says the weather is extreme and the people friendly. When she isn't writing romances, she enjoys horse racing and touring the countryside on a motorcycle.

Stella is very proud to know that she can give joy to others through her books. And now, thanks to the Oklahoma Library for the Blind in Oklahoma City, she is able to reach an even bigger audience. The library has transcribed her novels onto cassette tapes so that blind people across the state can also enjoy them.

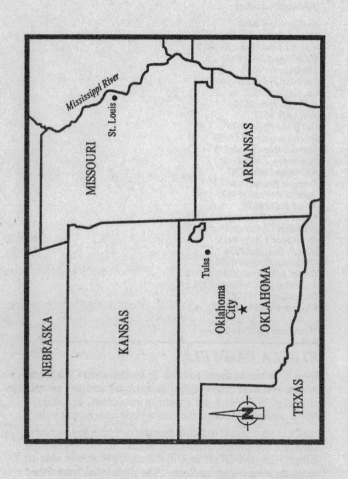

Chapter One

Lucas Lowrimore cursed as he glanced in the rearview mirror. A patrol car was right on his tail, and from the look of its flashing lights, the officer inside expected him to stop.

Great! Just great! He was already late for the game. Now the kids were bound to think he wasn't going to show at all!

Lucas pulled his black sports car alongside the curb and rolled down his window. While he waited for an officer to approach him, he dug his driver's license out of his wallet.

Moments later footsteps on the concrete street alerted him. Quickly Lucas poked his head out the open window and was immediately surprised to see a tall redheaded woman in a police uniform standing a couple of feet from his door.

"Please get out of the car, sir," she ordered.

"Is there a problem, Officer?" he asked, wondering how it had been his luck, or perhaps misfortune, to be stopped by a woman police officer. Not that a woman officer was something unique in the city. He'd seen many of them patrolling the streets, he'd just never been this close to one before.

"I'll tell you what the problem is when you get out of the car," she said, her deep voice carrying a note of warning.

Seeing no way to avoid the inevitable, Lucas unfolded his long frame from the sleek little car and stepped out on the concrete beside the redhead. "I know I was probably going a little fast through here," he started, "but—"

"I'd call fifteen miles past the limit more than a little fast," she said, then extended her palm toward him. "Let me see your license, sir."

Lucas handed her the plastic card while trying not to stare at her. but that was impossible not to do. Lucas had never seen a woman with a pistol strapped to her hips. And what hips they were, he thought, his brows unconsciously lifting with male appreciation as his eyes traveled down the long length of her.

"I'm—well, I'm in a hurry," he attempted to explain.

"You *were* in a hurry," she corrected, her full lips compressed to a disapproving line. "Did you know you ran a stop sign two blocks back?"

A stop sign? He'd never seen a stop sign! Still, that wasn't any reason not to get a ticket. "No. I wasn't aware of it. As I said, I'm late—"

"You should have started earlier," she said, her husky voice unyielding as she began scribbling on the clipboard resting against the crook of her arm. "Just where is this fire you're going to, Mr. Lowrimore?"

Lucas gritted his teeth and reminded himself it wouldn't help his cause if he pointed out to her that her mouth was just a little too smart for his taste.

"I'm going to a football game. And I've got less than twenty minutes to get there."

Jenny Prescott looked up from her clipboard and ran her eyes up and down his charcoal gray suit and maroon patterned tie. "Must be a new kind of football. I thought the players were the only ones who wore suits, not the spectators."

Who in hell did this woman think she was? So maybe he had been speeding a little and maybe he had missed a stop sign. That didn't mean he deserved a whiplashing with her spiked tongue.

"I'm not a spectator, I'm the coach."

Her eyes lifted to his face, and for the first time since she'd approached the sinfully expensive sports car, she allowed herself to really look at the driver's face. It was as impressive as his car and his clothes. Dark, nearly black hair was slicked back from his forehead. His eyes were brown, deep set and fringed with thick black lashes. His brows were equally black and at the moment pulled together in a frustrated frown. His lips were tugged downward at the corners, but Jenny got the impression they usually had a smile on them. A flirtatious one, she'd guess.

"That's too bad," she said.

Lucas's brows lifted higher, and Jenny noticed one of them had a faint white scar running through the middle of it.

"Why? Are you arresting me?"

Keeping her expression unreadable on the job had never been hard for Jenny to do. Until now. For some reason she had the insane urge to give this man a catty, taunting smile. He was obviously one of those men who thought his money gave him the right to break traffic regulations any time or any place. Well, this was one time she was certainly going to see that he paid for it.

"Give me a minute or two and I'll let you know," she said.

Jenny walked to the patrol car and leaned her head in the driver's window.

"Run this name and and number, Orville. He says he's on his way to a football game, but I want to make sure he hasn't just stolen that car."

The thin, mouse-brown-haired man reached for the two-way mike on the dash. "He looks like he could easily afford it, Jenny, but we'll make sure. Hey, this is—" He stopped reading the license to glance at Jenny. "This guy is Lucas T. Lowrimore!"

"Am I supposed to know who that is?"

"Jenny, that's Lucas T. Lowrimore!" Orville gushed as though he'd just stumbled onto a movie star. "You know, L.L. Freight. I've heard he was a young guy. Made all his money the old-fashioned way."

"You mean he inherited it?" Jenny muttered the question as she continued to write out the ticket.

"No. Like the commercial says. He earned it. Boy, what an entrepreneur. I'll bet women are always following him around!"

"Well, they'll not likely catch him if he continues to drive this fast," Jenny replied with obvious disgust.

"Well, you did," Orville pointed out.

Jenny gave her partner a droll look. "Run the license, Orville. It's hot as he—heck out here."

"Yes, ma'am. Just a minute and we'll know the goods on Mr. Lucas Lowrimore!" Orville assured her with his usual zest.

After the dispatcher came on the radio with the information Jenny needed, she walked over to the tall, dark trucking tycoon.

"Looks like everything checks out, Mr. Lowrimore. You won't be making a trip down to the station after all. But you will be making one to the courthouse."

"You're giving me a ticket?"

The surprise in his voice irked Jenny even more. Was she simply supposed to let him violate traffic laws and endanger people's lives because he was rich?

She handed him the slip of paper. "I hope in the future, Mr. Lowrimore, that you'll take into account the danger you're imposing on others when you speed down a residential street. If a child—"

Lucas was normally a laid-back man, and when he made mistakes he was always the first one to admit it, but something about this redhead with a gun on her hip and a badge on her breast stirred his blood. In more ways than one.

"I wasn't *racing* through here, Officer—" He glanced more closely at her badge. "Officer Prescott. I was, in spite of what you think, watching where I was going. And I would never intentionally endanger a child's life!"

She folded her arms across her breasts and gave him a just-keep-it-up look.

Angry now, Lucas said, "If you're through with me, I'll write you a check for the damages I've done and be on my way."

Jenny watched him reach inside his suit jacket for a checkbook. Jade cuff links glinted at his wrist while an onyx ring circled the fourth finger on his right hand. There was no ring on his left hand, and Jenny surmised he wasn't married, or if he was, he didn't want anyone knowing it.

"Sorry, I can't take your check," she told him. "It has to be cash."

His brown eyes turned to twin daggers. This woman obviously knew who he was. Or at least she had easy access to the information. Still, she insisted on treating him as if he was a potential criminal. "I don't normally carry—" he cast a disgusted eye at the ticket in his hand "—this sort of cash around with me."

Jenny gave him a purely professional smile. "I'm glad to see you follow *some* safety precautions, Mr. Lowrimore. Perhaps you'll include proper driving habits with them from now on."

The more she spoke, the more his eyes were drawn to her lips. They were dusky pink, soft and full. The kind Lucas would normally find extremely kissable. The thought had his gaze gliding up her straight nose and into her hazel green eyes. What would it be like to kiss Officer Prescott? he wondered dryly. About the same as trying to stroke a mountain lion, he figured.

"I'll do my best," he told her.

There was a glint of devilry shining in his brown eyes, and Jenny felt her hackles rise even higher. "See that you pay that fine on time, Mr. Lowrimore. And in the future, I suggest you keep a careful eye for traffic signs."

He smiled at her, a full-fledged smile that creased both his cheeks and lowered his thick black lashes. "Oh, rest assured, Officer Prescott, every time I look at one, I'll think of you."

For a moment, Jenny tried to think of some legal excuse to write him up again. But she couldn't think of a one, so she simply said, "See that you do."

Moments later, she slid into the patrol car. Orville took one look at her face and whistled under his breath.

"Boy, you look as mad as a hornet. What did he do? Get smart? Try to bribe you?"

Orville was frighteningly close to Mayberry's Barney Fife. He was skinny, homely and overeager. Jenny had never figured out how he'd managed to make it through the police academy. But somehow he had, and she'd had the incredible luck of being assigned his partner.

Yet there were good sides to working with Orville. He'd never consider making a pass at her, and he had a deep-seated kindness that made her overlook all his annoying habits.

Sighing, Jenny wiped her hand across her damp brow. "He didn't *do* anything. He was just—" She stopped, shook her head, then tried again. "I don't know, Orville. It was just the lazy way he got out of that car and then those clothes—"

"Sharp-looking, huh? I'll bet he didn't buy those off a rack."

Jenny's frown deepened, drawing her auburn brows close together. "He says he's on his way to coach a football game and he's late. I don't think we've ever heard that one, have we?"

Orville made a tsking noise with his tongue. "Now Jenny, you've been at this job long enough to learn you'll hear all sorts of stories when a person knows he's about to get a ticket."

That was true enough, Jenny thought. And what did it matter if he really wasn't going to a football game? As long as he didn't break the law, it was no concern of hers. Still, Jenny didn't like the idea of a well-to-do man like Lucas Lowrimore insulting her intelligence.

"Besides," Orville went on, "that suit of his might be his coaching clothes."

Jenny let out a snort as she watched the black, low-slung car pull slowly away from the curb. "When pigs fly."

Orville cut off the patrol car's flashing lights and pulled onto the street. "What do you say we go get something cold to drink? We've still got two more hours of duty, and nothing has been called in on the radio."

"Sounds good to me," Jenny told him. She needed something to cool her off.

Face it, Jenny, you need more than a cold drink to fix what ails you, she told herself as she stared out the window of the black and white patrol car. For the past month, ever since Savanna had told her she was pregnant, Jenny had felt restless, even forlorn. And that wasn't like her.

Her mood didn't make any sense at all. Savanna was her best friend, and she wanted her to be happy with her new family. But seeing her friend so much in love with her new husband had reminded Jenny of what her own life had become. She was thirty-three, almost thirty-four, and she had no one but herself.

Oh, she'd had a husband once, but Marcus hadn't been worth the paper their marriage license had been printed on. It had taken her five years to figure that out. Jenny had endured five years of mental, and sometimes physical, abuse before she'd finally realized that Marcus would never change, nor would he ever love her.

Nearly six years had passed since she'd kicked Marcus out of her house and her life. She'd never regretted it. He'd been bad for her, and to do anything else would have been to commit slow suicide. She knew that. She also knew that somewhere out there she could probably find a man who would be kind to her, who might even love her. But Marcus had made her too afraid to look. If she lived to be eighty she believed she'd still be afraid.

"Ya know, I've always wondered what it would feel like to be rich and famous like Lucas Lowrimore," Orville said a few moments later, after they'd purchased cold drinks and carried them to the patrol car. "Do you really think that sort of life is all it's cracked up to be?"

"I wouldn't know what sort of life Lucas Lowrimore has. An easy one, from the looks of it," Jenny told him.

After buckling her seat belt, she jammed the foam cup between her knees, then picked up the clipboard holding the ticket she'd written the man. Lucas T. Lowrimore, she read. Age thirty-five. Six foot three, two hundred and twenty pounds. Black hair, brown eyes. Address five minutes away from their present location.

"Looks like he lives just off North Pennsylvania," she murmured thoughtfully. "That's in our area. Want to drive by and take a look?"

"Do you?"

From the eager look on her partner's face, she knew anything but yes would be the wrong answer. The closest to fame that Orville would ever get was arresting a liquor store robber or a drunk down on Reno. Cops rarely became well-known or rich like Lucas Lowrimore, though that was all right with Jenny. She was proud of her job and the people she served. But since Orville liked to fantasize, it would give him a kick to see where trucking tycoon Lucas Lowrimore resided. And if Jenny was honest with herself, she was a little bit curious to see where the man lived, too. He hadn't been a routine traffic stop. At least not where she was concerned. She could still remember every little thing about the man. And all of it continued to nettle her.

"Sure, why not?" Jenny told him.

Five minutes later they were traveling down a street lined with elaborately landscaped lawns, massive brick homes and expensive cars parked in wide driveways.

"This is it," Jenny said as she carefully read off the house number. "I don't see his car. He's probably pulled it into the garage."

Orville slowed the patrol car to a crawl and looked out the windshield. "Boy howdy! How would you like to live in that?"

Jenny studied the L-shaped brick home. It was modest by Hollywood standards, she supposed, but seemed rich to her. She wondered if he stayed there very much, and if she went inside, would she find a wife and children waiting for him to come home?

She pulled her brows together in a faint frown. Lucas Lowrimore didn't have that married, family-man look about him. In fact, he'd looked like a smooth philanderer to Jenny.

"That's not my cup of tea, Orville. I want to live where I can put my feet on the furniture and eat in the living room if I want to." And she didn't want a man around telling her what to do. Or hitting her if she didn't do it.

Shaking his head, Orville drove on past the Lowrimore residence. "You're a hard one to figure, Jenny."

So she'd been told before, Jenny thought. But she wasn't about to change.

The two of them drove slowly through the quiet residential area, then turned and headed toward the main thoroughfare. They'd gone about five blocks when Jenny noticed a park full of kids. That wasn't unusual on a late fall evening. It was the car parked nearby that caught her attention.

"Stop, Orville!"

"What's the matter?" Frantically, he wheeled the car to the side of the street and reached to make a radio call.

"Put that down!" She grabbed the mike from his hand and hung it on the dash. "That's Lowrimore's car over there," she explained, inclining her head toward the black sports car.

Orville's skinny face swung toward the park. "Why, you're right."

Before she even realized what she was doing, Jenny climbed out of the patrol car and peered across the fifty yards or so to the group of children and the tall man they were clustered around.

It *was* Lucas Lowrimore! The football game he'd said he was hurrying to was obviously with these children.

For a moment Jenny felt like a complete heel. But only for a moment. As a police officer she was supposed to doubt and never assume that a person was telling her the truth.

From this distance she could see that he'd taken off the gray jacket and rolled the sleeves of his white shirt above his elbows. A football was tucked beneath his left arm while his right hand was busy pointing to specific children.

What was a man like that doing with a bunch of ragamuffin children?

The sight so intrigued Jenny she was still thinking about it when she got home later that night. Yet by bedtime she'd convinced herself it didn't matter what Lowrimore was doing coaching football on a playground in the park. He'd simply been one of hundreds of traffic violators she and Orville stopped throughout the year. In her line of work she met all kinds.

The next morning she was dressing when the telephone rang. She walked over to the nightstand by her bed, tossed back her long red hair and picked up the receiver.

"Prescott here," she answered quickly.

A female voice at the other end of the line giggled, and Jenny knew immediately that it was her friend Savanna. "Jenny, you sound so official," she said.

"That's the way I'm supposed to sound," Jenny replied, laughing along with her. "How would it sound if the police chief called me and I answered 'hiya, honey'?"

Savanna laughed again, then groaned miserably. "Oh, don't do this to me so early in the morning. I haven't eaten my crackers yet."

"Still having morning sickness?" Jenny asked with concern.

"Not nearly as much as before. I'm getting through it. Besides, it's all worth it to have Joe's child."

Jenny eased down on the side of the bed. "You must love that oilman a whole lot."

"I do," the other woman said with a contented sigh that made Jenny wonder what kind of man it would take to make her feel that way. "But right now," Savanna went on, "I'm wondering if you'd like to come over for supper. We're going to barbecue out by the pool. Dad and Gloria have driven up for a visit, and I thought you might like to join in on the family fun."

Family fun? Jenny didn't know what that was. She'd never known her daddy. As for her mother, she'd hardly been the cookie-baking, bedtime-story-reading type. While Jenny had grown up, Ruby Prescott had worked in a bar, smoked like a chimney and cursed like a sailor. In fact, Ruby was still living in a little town west of Fort Stockton, Texas, working in the same tavern and reminiscing about the smooth charmer who'd seduced her all those years ago and gotten her pregnant with Jenny.

Twice a year Jenny went to see her mother. But she never stayed more than three or four days at a time. Just long enough to assure herself that Ruby didn't need her.

Actually, Ruby had never needed her daughter and never would. So when Savanna talked about family fun, Jenny could only wonder and wish.

"Sorry, Savanna. I've got duty tonight. But thanks for asking."

"Oh, darn!" Savanna said with obvious disappointment. "How about coming over for breakfast then?"

"Now? I thought you had morning sickness."

Savanna laughed. "By ten o'clock that will be gone and I'll be ready for pancakes and peanut butter."

"Oh, Lord, I'm the one who's going to be sick now," Jenny said.

"You can have yours with plain ol' artery-clogging butter," Savanna suggested.

"Sorry again, love. I'm going to court this morning. I've got to meet with the DA about a manslaughter trial."

"Oh, a murder case?"

Jenny reached for the coffee cup she'd left on the nightstand. After a quick sip, she answered, "You might call it that. The guy got behind the wheel of a pickup with his blood full of alcohol. At the I-40 exit on May Avenue he smashed into a car and killed two people."

Savanna said, "Do your best to put him behind bars, Jen. I don't want anyone like him endangering my children's lives."

I would never intentionally endanger a child.

From out of nowhere Lucas Lowrimore's words popped into her head, and for a moment she considered telling her friend about stopping the sexy-looking businessman who drove too fast. But she didn't. Savanna was always hunting for a potential mate for Jenny. It would be just like her to call the man and ask if he was available!

"I will," Jenny promised. "And call me soon."

* * *

As Jenny drove to the courthouse she noticed it was going to be another warm autumn day. White clouds moved lazily from the south to the north, and the first yellow leaves from the elms and hickory were beginning to fall and scatter across the lawns and sidewalks.

Too bad she didn't have the day off, she thought. It might be nice to ride her bicycle over to the lake, take a sandwich with her and extra bread for the ducks. But she had to work, and anyway she couldn't think of a soul who might want to go with her.

There I go with that lonely-little-Jenny stuff again, she silently scolded herself. What was the matter with her? Just because she would turn thirty-four in a few days didn't mean she had to start feeling sorry for herself.

She should be feeling as chipper as a songbird. Her birthday was on Halloween, and this year the police department was throwing a huge charity dance for the needy children of the city. It was going to be a big event with live music, lots of food and all sorts of people attending. She'd never had a birthday party before. So this was one night she thoroughly intended to enjoy. And no more whining about being alone, she firmly reminded herself.

A few minutes later, she arrived at the courthouse parking lot. As usual, all the spaces were filled. She made one pass through the rows of cars, then started on a second. If she didn't find one this time, she'd be forced to park down the street and walk back. Which would make her have to hurry. Her meeting began in fifteen minutes, and the DA frowned on anyone creeping into his office late.

Suddenly, a black car emerged unexpectedly from a parking slot directly in front of her. She pressed down on the horn, at the same time jamming on the brakes as hard as she could.

All four tires squealed loudly on the pavement, and the hood bounced up and down as Jenny's car finally came to a halt a few inches from the driver's door.

"Idiot!" She cursed under her breath.

"What the hell! That crazy driver nearly hit me," Lucas muttered. He jerked the safety belt away from his waist and climbed out the passenger door of the car.

"It's you!" Jenny gasped at the tall, dark-haired man rounding the rear of the black car. "I should have known!"

Lucas's head whipped around and he saw *her!* The red-head! It was impossible not to recognize her. Even when she was out of uniform, he knew the curvy shape of her body and that flaming red hair billowing around her face and shoulders.

"You nearly hit me!" he countered as he stalked the few steps that separated them. "What were you doing flying through here like that?"

Flying? She hadn't even been going five miles per hour. "I was hardly flying, Mr. Lowrimore. What were you doing? Trying to get a ticket for speeding in reverse?"

She couldn't write him up again. At least Lucas didn't think so. She was apparently off duty and without that little metal clipboard she'd scribbled his ticket on.

"Actually, I'm late again."

Jenny didn't know what it was, but something about this man made adrenaline surge through her body like a summer squall.

Raking her eyes up and down the muscled length of him, she said, "Well, I can see you're not dressed for football this morning."

He was wearing faded jeans, cowboy boots and a mustard-colored long-sleeved shirt. The clothes fit him as well as the suit he'd been wearing, and she knew if Orville could see him now he'd be just as impressed with the man as he had been last night. Thank goodness, she wasn't!

He gave her a crinkly-eyed smile, and Jenny's gaze was drawn to the faint dimples in his cheeks and the slightly crooked line of his white teeth.

"I'm on my way to work," he told her, then realized she was the first woman in a long time he'd bothered to explain his comings and goings to. And he wouldn't have done it now, except that she was a police officer. And for some damn stupid reason he wanted to tell her.

Jenny's gaze swept over his broad shoulders and trim waist. The man wore suits to football games and jeans to work. He was obviously rich, yet he'd been playing football with a bunch of street kids. What sort of man was he, anyway? she wondered.

The kind you need to stay away from, Jenny.

"Oh, I see," she said aloud. "This morning you have a different excuse for your reckless driving habits."

He smiled at her again, only this time there was an odd sort of gleam in his eye that made Jenny want to place a protective hand over her bosom.

"Not really. I'm running late, just like last night. Although, I wouldn't be late this morning if a certain officer had been kind enough to give me a warning ticket instead of the real thing. Then I wouldn't have needed to make this trip to the courthouse."

She was glad to hear she'd at least inconvenienced him. She smiled. "You look like a man who appreciates the *real thing*."

Dear Lord, this woman got to him. Lucas didn't understand it. After last night, he'd never expected to see her again. Even so, he'd lost several hours of sleep wondering where she lived, if she was married and why he should even care. Now, this morning, she'd very nearly run into him. Yet at this moment he was exhilarated by the simple sight of her.

Drawing in a deep breath, Lucas shifted his weight from one booted foot to the other and looked down at the pink color creeping across her cheeks. "Where are you going this fine morning, Officer Prescott? I see you're without your gun and badge."

And Jenny felt naked. She didn't know whether that was because she was out of uniform or because Lucas Lowrimore was looking at her the way a man looks at a woman and likes what he sees.

She glanced at her watch. "I hope to be in the DA's office in seven minutes."

He shoved back the cuff of his shirt and peered at his watch. "Damn, I'm going to be late, too. Let me pull out of the way so you can park your car."

Lucas climbed into his car. Before he could shut the door, however, *she* leaned her head in the window.

"Yes?" he questioned.

"I, uh, I just wanted to tell you that I saw you with the kids last night. You weren't lying to me about the football game."

His dark brows arched with dry amusement. "You doubted my story?"

Her nostrils flared daintily. "That's what I'm trained to do, Mr. Lowrimore. So if I offended you, well, that's just part of my job."

That almost sounded like an apology, Lucas thought. He didn't get many of those. Especially from women. Most of the ones he knew where too busy wanting and demanding to consider his feelings.

"Thank you for that, Officer Prescott."

She gave him a little smile, then turned away from the car. She'd already said more than she should have to the man. She had to get to work and put Lucas T. Lowrimore out of her mind for good.

His car engine started, then his voice rose above it.

"Uh—Officer Prescott," he called out.

She looked at him over her shoulder, then wished she hadn't. He was smiling at her. One of those dangerous, masculine smiles that made a woman forget she had a brain or how to use it.

"Yes?" she asked, not bothering to hide the wariness in her voice.

"You haven't told me your first name."

What difference did it make? Jenny wondered. She'd never see the man again. Unless she caught him speeding.

"It's Jenny," she said.

Still smiling, his eyes held hers. "Well, Officer Jenny Prescott, are you married?"

The question took her aback, and then she let out a throaty laugh. "Not even in my dreams, Mr. Lowrimore."

Lucas watched her turn and walk to her car, his eyes appreciating every little jiggle of her body.

She might be a police officer. And she might give his peace of mind all sorts of trouble. But she was all woman. And he suddenly knew he had to have her.

Chapter Two

"Not even in my dreams, Mr. Lowrimore."

Two days later Lucas was still pondering Jenny Prescott's words. What had she really meant, he wondered for the umpteenth time. Obviously she wasn't married. Nor did she want to be. But did that mean she didn't want to be married in general? Or more specifically married to someone like him?

Hell, Lucas, why are you even thinking such things? he asked himself. A year ago marriage hadn't even been in his vocabulary. He was a bona fide bachelor. He was his own boss, he lived alone, and he liked it that way. Or at least he thought he did. However, more and more he was beginning to ask himself if that was the way he wanted to spend the rest of his life.

Frustrated with his thoughts, Lucas rose from the wide desk and walked to the window that overlooked part of the truck yard. Tractors and semitrailers were lined neatly across the tarmac, the words L.L. Freight emblazoned across the side of each rig in bright red letters.

L.L. Freight, he silently repeated. That was him. He'd built the business from the ground up, with nothing but a worn-out rig and his own two hands to drive it. Now he had scores of trucks and drivers and so many hauling orders they could hardly keep up with them.

In the past ten years he'd made money. Lots of it. But he still didn't feel rich. Truth was, Lucas had never set out to make himself rich. He was just a man who liked to work, and the fruits of his labor had paid off.

Lucas was proud of his business. He'd be crazy not to be. Especially in these days and times, when the economy could take a nosedive at any moment. But in the past year he'd come to realize there was a hole in his life.

Years ago, when he'd been young and poor and uncertain about where his life was headed, he'd thought money would fix everything. Not a lot of money. Just enough to pay his bills and make him comfortable. Now he had more money than he'd probably ever spend, and he didn't feel fixed or comfortable. He felt restless. He felt alone and he felt old.

There was a light knock on the door. "Come in."

A petite woman in her early seventies with beehive blond hair and black rhinestone-studded glasses walked into the room.

"I've finally managed to locate Mr. Johnson," she said. "He'll be in touch with you by the end of the week."

"Mr. Johnson?" he repeated blankly.

The secretary shot him an impatient look. "The insurance man who says he can save you thousands on liability costs."

"Oh, yes, the insurance guy. Good work." Lucas walked to the front of his desk and took a seat on the corner. "Lilah, are you an honest woman?"

The older woman slid the rhinestone glasses to the end of her nose and batted her false eyelashes as she looked at her boss.

"If you're referring to my relationships with men, then you know, Mr. Lowrimore, that I've—well—known two or three men since I've been working for you. But none of them made an honest woman of me."

Even though Lilah was outrageously flamboyant, she was a sweetheart. And a hell of a secretary. He couldn't run the place without her, and they both knew it. As far as her boyfriends went, Lucas figured she'd had more than a dozen or so in the past few years. But he wasn't going to be the one to point that out to her.

"I'm not talking about that, Lilah. I'm asking if you're truthful with people when they ask you an opinion." ·

"Oh, well," she said, pushing her glasses up her nose and clearing her throat, "in that case, I'm brutally honest."

Lucas folded his arms across his chest. "Then tell me, Lilah, am I old?"

She took a step closer, gave him a lusty look, then shook her head. "Mr. Lowrimore, if you're old, then I wish I were, too."

A frown twisted his mouth. "You're just looking at the outside, Lilah. You can't see how I'm feeling on the inside."

Shaking her head, Lilah walked to his desk and began to straighten the clutter. "You're just tired, honey. You've been trying to do too much here lately. It's no wonder you're feeling old. Why, between this place and those children's shelters, I don't know how you have any sanity left."

"I'm not tired, Lilah." He was empty, deep-down empty. And he didn't know why. "As far as those shelters go, they're very important to me."

She tossed a half-eaten sandwich into the trash. "I know they are. But you need relaxation of your own. You need a—"

"Woman," he finished for her, wondering how many times he'd heard this from his secretary. Actually, Lilah was the closest thing to a mother he'd ever had, and he valued her opinion. He just didn't always agree with it.

"Well, I've met a woman," he added.

"Dear Lord," Lilah said, pressing her palms together and lifting her eyes to the ceiling.

Lucas shook his head in wry disbelief. "You don't need to pray about it, Lilah."

"I'm not praying, I'm giving thanks." She looked at her boss. "So when are you going to see her again? What is she like?"

A crooked grin on his face, Lucas held up a hand. "I don't really know her—yet. She's a policewoman."

"Oh."

"What does that mean? She's not a leper."

Lilah shot him a sarcastic look. "I wasn't implying anything of the sort. I just remember that story you told me about losing your policeman friend. Knowing that, I can't see you getting close to anyone who's a target for that sort of danger."

Lilah was right. Given a choice, he'd never intentionally look twice at a woman who worked as a law officer. But in this case, he couldn't seem to help himself. He desperately wanted to see Jenny again. "Well, it's not like I plan to get that *close* to her, Lilah. And you've been saying I needed a little female companionship."

"So I did. What's this police officer's name?"

"Jenny Prescott. And that's about all I know. Other than that she's a gorgeous redhead."

Lilah's expression turned incredulous. Whipping her glasses off, she stared at him. "That's all you know?"

"Give me time, Lilah! I've got to think of some way to make our paths cross again."

The words were barely out of his mouth, and Lucas could see the wheels starting to turn in his secretary's head.

"Maybe she likes to dance," Lilah suggested after a moment. "You're going to the policeman's charity Halloween dance tonight, aren't you?"

The charity dance! He'd forgotten all about it. "Damn it, Lilah, why didn't you mention the dance this morning?"

"Because you've been talking about it for days now. I hardly thought it necessary to remind you."

He glanced at his watch. "Do I have any meetings left?"

Lilah shook her head. "There's nothing of real importance left on your calendar today. Go on. I'll take care of everything here."

Lucas patted her cheek and hurried toward the door.

"You take care of things with that redhead," she called after him. "But take care you watch that heart of yours, hear?"

Laughing, Lucas stepped into the corridor of the office building. "I'll do my best, Lilah." He spoke the words over his shoulder.

Later that night, Jenny stood at the edge of the large crowd, watching couples circle the makeshift dance floor. The Halloween charity dance had started inside the municipal building, but the weather turned out to be mild and clear, and every available officer had pitched in to move the party outside to the parking lot. And from the looks of things, all the hard work had been worth it. People were still arriving and dropping money into the giant jar set up at the entrance.

Tapping her toe to an old Bruce Springsteen number, Jenny suddenly felt a hand on her shoulder. Expecting it to be Orville, she looked around, then stared in total surprise at Lucas Lowrimore.

"Oh, it's you," she said with a little gasp.

He grinned at her as his eyes scanned her face. "Who were you expecting, the devil?"

Her brows lifted at his question and then she smiled. "I may look witchy tonight, Mr. Lowrimore, but that doesn't mean I'm expecting Lucifer to show his face around here."

Lucas's gaze traveled from the top of her auburn hair to the black high-heeled boots peeking from the hem of her long skirt. She looked anything but witchy to him.

"This crowd is huge," he said above the noise of the music. "It took me a long time to find you."

Once again surprise was etched upon her face. "You were looking for me?"

He nodded as he admired the thick wave of hair dipping over her eye. The rest of it was tied at her nape with a wide, black velvet ribbon. He knew if he was to reach up and pull one end of the bow, the red mass of waves would come tumbling around her shoulders. For one wild moment, he considered doing it just to see the outrage on her pretty face.

"You're the only police person I know."

"Then what are you doing here?"

Lucas laughed at her point-blank question. "Why, I'm here for the children. Isn't everyone?"

Of course, Jenny thought, as embarrassed color swept across her cheeks. But the way he'd said he'd been hunting her—well, it had led her mind in other directions. Crazy directions, so it seemed.

"I hope so. That is why my precinct is putting this dance on. By the way, you can drop more money into the jar before you leave—if you want to, that is," she added.

"I already have. A check from my trucking company."

She nodded, then turned her attention to the dancers. He was the last person she'd expected to see here tonight. In fact, after that day in the courthouse parking lot, she hadn't ever expected to see him again. Having him standing here beside her as if she was an old acquaintance was making her downright giddy.

"I'm sure the children will appreciate it. And believe me there's plenty of them who need help," she replied.

"I know," he said, then curled his fingers around her upper arm.

A jolt of crackling fire raced to her shoulder. Jenny tried to ignore it as she looked questioningly at him.

"Would you like a glass of punch?" he asked.

Jenny nodded. Her mouth was as dry as straw, and she didn't have a good excuse not to go with him. Other than the fear of making a fool of herself, and she could hardly admit that to him.

Jenny wasn't good around men. Not in a one-on-one, personal kind of situation. She hadn't always been that way. In fact, during high school and two years of junior college, she'd enjoyed being around young men. But then she'd met and married Marcus, and he'd shown her a different side of the male species. Now she could rarely look at a man without wondering what dark, evil part of him was hiding behind his smile.

"My partner, Orville, said you owned a trucking firm here in the city," she said moments later as Lucas handed her a cold glass of fruit punch.

Lucas nodded as he filled himself a glass from the huge punch bowl. "If you'd known that before you started writing my ticket, would it have made a difference? For the better, that is?"

Jenny found herself laughing in spite of her nervousness. "Not in the least. I don't show partiality to anyone."

"Not even your family?" he countered jokingly.

"I don't have family—around here," she replied flatly.

"Oh." It was all he could say, which was ridiculous when he thought about it. Lucas had never been at a loss for words in his life. But something about the look on her face, the shadowy wall in her eyes had unsettled him.

"Do you have family here?" she asked after a few moments.

Lucas shook his head, and Jenny thought she'd never seen a man whose presence was quite so interwoven with his looks and his deep voice. Taken apart feature by feature, he wasn't all that handsome a man. His nose was large, his complexion a bit rough, his face too lean. But put together with his sleek, dark hair, his rock-hard body and crooked smile, he was dangerous.

He was a man who touched a woman in the innermost part of her. In one word, he was sexy. He might not know it. But Jenny did. And having him stand next to her, his shoulder inadvertently brushing hers, was playing havoc with her breathing reflexes.

"I'm an only child," he told her. "And my father, the only family I have left, lives near the Florida Everglades in an old houseboat with a bunch of snakes and gators for neighbors."

"Sounds dangerous," Jenny said.

Lucas laughed. "Dad would enjoy hearing a woman like you say that. He always did consider himself an adventurer."

A woman like her? What did he mean by that? Jenny wondered. Slanting her hazel green eyes at him, she studied his dark face, made even darker by the navy blue turtleneck he was wearing.

He was a man who laughed easily. As if laughter came naturally to him. Had his life always been filled with laughter? Had he never had to worry, to make sacrifices or endure the pain of loss? She definitely had too many questions about the man, she scolded herself.

But that didn't stop her from asking another one. "What about you, Mr. Lowrimore? Are you an adventurer?"

The band began to play "Hungry Heart." Jenny silently sang along with the words. Because they fit her. They'd always fit her.

Lucas shrugged. "I used to be."

She continued to look at him, and Lucas realized she was waiting for him to say more. He wasn't sure he wanted to. This woman was a cop, and long ago he'd made a vow never to get close to an officer of the law. But she was so different, so tempting. In spite of his vow and in spite of her being a policewoman, he wanted to get to know her.

"I was in the marines when I was young," he told her after a moment. "That was extremely adventurous. After my time was up, I came out into the civilian world looking for something to get into. So I bought a run-down tractor-trailer rig from my father and spent some time driving cross-country. The rest, as they say, is history."

"That must be quite a story, from one truck to owning a large company," she said, deliberately turning her eyes to the dancers.

"I worked hard, invested my money and had a little luck with me. Things turned out good."

The music changed, and once again, Jenny felt Lucas's hand on her arm. "Would you like to dance?"

She'd expected him to drink his punch, making a little small talk and move off into the crowd. It wasn't turning out that way, and Jenny didn't know whether to be wary or thrilled that he was paying her so much attention.

"I'm not that much of a dancer."

"I saw you dancing earlier. You looked like you were doing all right then."

Jenny blushed. "That was Orville, my partner. He's about as surefooted as I am, and that's not saying much."

He took the cup from her hand and tossed it along with his into a nearby trash barrel. Then taking her by the hand, he led her out among the dancing crowd. The music had slowed to a bluesy number, and Jenny reluctantly went into his arms.

For long moments neither one of them said anything, and Jenny felt a strange sort of panic come over her. She was trained to deal with all sorts of dangerous situations, but none of that training was helping her to deal with Lucas Lowrimore. What was he doing here with her? Dancing with her? He was rich, handsome and not someone who traveled in her social circle. Was he simply amusing himself with her company on a warm Halloween night?

"Are you familiar with some of the other charity work we do for children?" she asked, hoping conversation between them would stop the warm rush of excitement she felt at being in his arms.

"I know that you have a toy drive at Christmas and a huge Easter egg hunt."

His dark gaze was sliding gently over her face. Jenny felt his touch as surely as if it had been his fingers, and she had to steel herself to keep from shivering with reaction.

Nodding, she said, "We also have a food drive around Thanksgiving, and that usually brings good results."

"God knows, there's plenty of kids around here who need food." He shook his head. "It's hard to believe, isn't it? That children go hungry in all countries, even ours."

Marcus had never wanted children. A fact he'd deliberately kept hidden from Jenny until after they were married. When she discovered his true feelings on the subject, she'd been devastated. She'd always dreamed of having children. But during their marriage, she'd put those dreams aside and taken great care not to get pregnant. She'd been afraid Marcus's unpredictable temper might have eventually turned on the child, and she could never have borne living under that sort of fear.

"Do you have any children, Mr. Lowrimore?"

"My name is Lucas. Call me that, would you? I already feel old enough."

She couldn't prevent a faint smile from crossing her face as she looked at him. "All right, Lucas."

"In answer to your question," he went on, "I don't have any children. But I like them. I like being around them. And I hate what today's society is doing to them."

A couple she knew danced by them. They waved at her and Jenny waved back, then she glanced at Lucas. "Such as?" she prompted.

"Such as making it impossible for a family to make ends meet unless both parents work. The fast life, the TV and video games. It's ruining their bodies and their minds. A lot of kids don't or can't use either one."

The music changed once again. This time the tempo was even slower, and Jenny wanted to protest when he pulled her closer against him. But she didn't. She wasn't a prude. She was a thirty-four-year-old woman. And what was it going to hurt if, for one night, she acted like one?

"The kids I saw you playing ball with the other day, how did you come to be doing that?" she asked curiously.

He chuckled and Jenny could feel his chest move against her breast. It was a tantalizing feeling and one that reminded Jenny how long it had been since a man had made love to her.

"A swarm of them used to play in the streets," Lucas explained. "And every evening on my way home from work, I'd have to stop the car and wait for them to clear out of the way. Finally, one evening I got out and laid the law down to them. I threatened to report them to the police, and if they didn't like that they could meet me in the park the next evening to discuss it. They agreed to be there, and I surprised them by showing up with a football. That was two years ago. Some of the names and faces have changed, but my reason for doing it hasn't."

Stirred in spite of herself, she asked, "And what is that?"

"To keep them off the streets and let them know that someone cares."

The texture of his palm was tough against hers. It made Jenny wonder what he did during the day and in his spare time. He obviously didn't have to do manual labor to make a living.

"Hey, Jenny, happy birthday!"

Jenny glanced around at the female voice to see her captain and his wife dancing a few feet away from them. She smiled at the older couple.

"Thank you, Valerie, and thank *you*, Captain Morgan, for throwing me such a huge party."

The gray-haired man gave her a little salute. "I try to keep my officers happy."

"Today is your birthday?" Lucas asked after the couple had danced past them. "Why didn't you say something?"

Jenny didn't understand this man or what he was really after. He'd walked up to her and acted like he'd known her for years. When in actuality he knew nothing about her except that she was a policewoman and she'd written him a hefty ticket.

"At my age, it's not something you go around announcing," she told him, recalling the black balloons and dead-looking weeds her fellow officers had given her today. She'd gotten a few crude birthday cards, too, and she'd laughed at them all. At least she'd been remembered. It had been at least ten years since she'd received so much as a card from her mother. It had made her feel too old to remember she had a grown daughter, Ruby had always said.

"Your age?" Lucas asked wryly. "Just what is your age?

She frowned at him. "I'm sure you know it's impolite to ask a woman that question."

He chuckled and Jenny's eyes were drawn to the gleam of his teeth and the dimples in his cheeks.

"Do you think that matters to me?"

His question, his laughter and the faint curve to his lips sent warning signals shivering down her spine. He was getting too cocky, too personal, and she'd danced with him far longer than she should have.

"I'm getting—winded," she said coolly. "If you'll excuse me, I think I'll go sit down."

To his utter dismay, Jenny twisted out of his arms and walked off into the crowd of onlookers lining the edge of the dance floor.

Muttering a curse to himself, he plunged into the crowd to find her.

Once she was away from the dance floor, Jenny slipped off into the darkness and didn't stop until she'd walked several yards across a wide lawn. A white wrought-iron park bench sat empty beneath a huge sycamore tree.

Jenny brushed the fallen leaves from the seat, then sank down with a sigh of relief. This night wasn't turning out to be anything like she'd expected. That she would see Lucas Lowrimore here tonight had never entered her mind. And even if it had, she would have never pictured herself dancing and conversing with the man.

Closing her eyes, she covered her face with her hands. Her cheeks were hot and her heart was pounding. And she was furious with herself. It was stupid—pure foolishness to let Lucas affect her like this.

Dear Lord, she thought with a sudden sinking realization. She was already thinking of him as Lucas!

"I don't know why you had to run off mad like that."

Jenny's heart stopped at the sound of his voice. Slowly she looked up to see him standing a step or two in front of her.

His hands were jammed in the back pockets of his jeans, causing the thin jersey of his turtleneck to stretch tautly across his chest. Jenny unconsciously swallowed at the sight of the wall of muscles bulging against the fabric.

"I—" Why had he followed her? It was crazy to think he wanted her company. The man probably had a whole bevy of women stashed across the state. Why bother with someone like her? Drawing in a bracing breath, she said, "I wasn't mad."

"Oh. I see. You were just a little irritated."

She glanced at his face. Amusement crinkled his eyes and curved the corners of his mouth. Jenny couldn't ever remember the sight of a man affecting her as much as this one was doing.

"No—well, yes," she stuttered.

Amused by her flustered attitude, Lucas chuckled as he took a seat beside her on the narrow bench. "You know, you really shouldn't be so touchy about your age. You look very young."

The sincerity in his voice melted her irritation and she slanted her eyes over to him.

"I'm thirty-four," she admitted. "And I'm not *touchy* about my age. I just don't like telling it to—"

"A stranger?" he finished for her.

Surprised by his insight, she nodded.

"Well, I don't mind telling a beautiful redheaded stranger that I'm thirty-five."

She grimaced. "Of course you don't mind. You knew I'd already read your age on your driver's license."

With a contented sigh, he stretched out his long legs and folded his arms across his chest. "I didn't expect you'd remember anything about me. I must have left more of an impression than I thought."

Wishing she could bite off her tongue, Jenny retorted, "Oh, you definitely left an impression. Believe me. I was desperately trying to think of some reason to give you another ticket. One that would hold up in court," she added.

He laughed and Jenny wondered why the sound sent little curls of longing shooting through her. She was always sharing jokes with her male friends, and she heard their laughter all the time. Why should Lucas be any different? Because when he laughed, it was warm and intimate and made her believe it was just for her, she realized.

"At least you're honest," he said.

Suddenly she shot him a daring glance. "Are you?"

"I try to be."

Turning her gaze over the empty lawn, Jenny let out a long breath. "Then why did you really come here tonight, Lucas? You could have mailed your contribution check. And I'm sure you have plenty of—things to keep you busy."

Lucas hadn't expected such a blunt question from her. But then, he supposed he should have. She wasn't a teenager. She was a mature woman, one who obviously didn't dance around the issue.

"I always have plenty of *things* to occupy my time. But I wanted to find you," he conceded.

Even though Jenny had suspected as much, just hearing him confirm it out loud very nearly knocked the wind from her. It had been months—no, years—since a man had pursued her in any fashion. She wasn't ready for it. She'd never be ready for it. He might as well know that right now.

"To tell me you've been working on your defensive driving?" she asked in the lightest voice she could muster.

"No. To ask you out to dinner."

"And what if I hadn't been here?"

He chuckled again as though he was enjoying himself immensely. "I would have gone back to my old speeding habits, and you and your little metal clipboard would have found me."

She snorted. "Well, you wasted your time. I usually work nights."

"There is a noonday meal called lunch," he suggested.

Jenny forced her eyes to meet his. "Look, Lucas, I don't go out with men. It's that simple."

He didn't look surprised. Intrigued was more like it.

"I'm not going to bother asking you why. I'm just going to tell you that you might as well get ready for that to change."

The pure male arrogance of his words sent fury flashing through Jenny like a streak of hot lightning. Her green eyes blazed with fire as she jumped to her feet and looked at him.

"I do have to follow orders on the job," she said quietly, "but I'll be damned before I do it anywhere else. Good night, Mr. Lowrimore."

Lucas watched her stalk angrily across the brown lawn and disappear into the crowd of partygoers. This time he didn't intend to go after her. He'd let her think she'd won tonight. But tomorrow, well, that was a whole different thing.

Lucas Lowrimore wasn't a quitter. He went after what he wanted and he usually got it. Officer Jenny Prescott was soon going to learn that.

Chapter Three

A bouquet of red roses was on Jenny's cluttered desk when she arrived at work the next afternoon. Jenny never received flowers. She couldn't imagine why she was getting them now, unless Ruby had experienced a change of heart and decided to say a belated happy birthday in an extravagant way. But hell freezing over would be more likely than that, Jenny thought ruefully.

Easing down on the heavy wooden chair at her desk, she pulled out the small square envelope attached to the flowers, then gasped as her eyes scanned the note she discovered inside.

> Red and prickly, these roses are just like you, Jenny.
> I hope you enjoy them as much as I did your company last night.
>
> Lucas

Jenny read the words through three times before she finally lifted her head and looked at the two dozen rose buds arranged in a cut crystal vase.

The man was incredible! What had she done to deserve this unwanted attention? What was she going to do to stop it?

"Wow! What beautiful roses. Did you get those for your birthday?"

Jenny glanced at the female officer who worked as Captain Morgan's secretary. "Uh—yes, Glenda, these are from a ... friend of mine."

Quickly Jenny slipped the card into the front pocket of her trousers. "Did you need me for something?"

The petite blonde nodded. "Captain Morgan wants to see you before you leave on patrol duty."

"About what? Do you know?"

Shaking her head, Glenda gave her a sly smile. "I'm sure it's not to give you more roses like those."

Jenny sighed and got to her feet. She might as well see her boss before she started doing her daily reports.

Captain Morgan was on the telephone when Jenny stepped into his office. He motioned for her to take a seat, then ended the call with a hard bang on the receiver.

"I hope that wasn't Valerie's eardrum you just busted," she said.

The older man chuckled ruefully. "No, the mayor's. And I hope he got the message. He thinks every person brought before a judge should be found guilty, and if they're not, it's our fault." The weary, gray-haired captain waved dismissively. "Enough about that. I wanted to tell you that I've assigned you a speaking engagement for Friday afternoon. Don't worry about Orville, I'll send Donald Coleman out with him."

The news made Jenny's mouth drop open, and she scooted to the edge of her seat. "A speaking engagement?

I haven't done anything like that in—it's probably been a year or more. Captain, I really don't—''

"I don't want any arguments about this, Jenny. It's only giving a safety lesson to a group of truck drivers. And you know how important these things are. The more drivers we can reach, the safer our public highways are.''

Jenny knew her boss was right, but she'd never felt comfortable speaking to a group of any sort. "Why me? Jim Everly is the one who does all those things. Send him.''

Captain Morgan shook his head. "The owner of the trucking firm asked specifically for you.''

A puzzled frown creased her face. "He did?''

The older officer nodded. "Yes. And when you're talking about a man with that much clout in the trucking business and our city, I don't want to disappoint him just because you're reluctant to do your job.''

"Who are you talking about?'' she asked, as wariness began to creep over her like a dark cloud.

"Lucas Lowrimore. L.L. Freight Company. He said you gave him a ticket and a lecture that he'd never forget. And he thinks his men will respond and listen to you better than they would a man.''

Jenny was suddenly seething. How dare Lucas Lowrimore use her job to get to her! It was indecent! Underhanded! And she was certainly going to tell him about it.

"I see,'' she said, her mind spinning with thoughts of retaliation. "So where and when do I give this lecture?''

He pushed a piece of paper toward her. "There's all the details you'll need. His secretary's name is Lilah, and she'll be available to assist you in any way.''

Jenny rose to her feet. "I'll do my best, Captain.''

He smiled at her. "I'm sure you will, Jenny. It's not in you to do anything else.''

* * *

The large house was dark when Jenny pulled into the driveway and parked beside Lucas's black sports car. Glancing at her watch, she decided the man surely didn't go to bed before ten. And if he did, that was too bad. She had something to say to him.

A footlight illuminated the small alcove sheltering the front entrance of the house. Jenny ran through the steady drizzle, then shook the water droplets from her hair as she stepped up to the door and punched the doorbell. Inside she could hear the muted sound of the chimes, and eventually footsteps.

Jenny rubbed her palms against her hips, then moistened her lips as she waited for him to open the door.

"Well, it's Officer Jenny Prescott," he said, his voice full of pleasure. "What a nice surprise."

He didn't look a bit surprised, Jenny thought, making her wonder if her being here was just what he'd planned. "I want to talk to you," she said bluntly.

A grin on his face, he pushed the door wide. "Please come in. I was just making myself a snack. Want to join me?"

She followed him through a large dark room that she assumed was the living room, then down a short hallway and into a brightly lit kitchen.

"No, thank you," she told him.

He glanced at her, then went to the counter where several food items sat near a wooden cutting board. "That's too bad. I just bought some great summer sausage."

Didn't he know she wanted to yell and scream at him, not eat summer sausage? "I've already eaten this afternoon."

He picked up a small butcher knife, then looked over his shoulder at her. "Are you off duty now?"

"A few minutes ago," she told him.

His dark eyes traveled up and down the length of her. "And you didn't even take time to go home and change before you came to see me. I wouldn't have expected such eagerness from you."

She knew he was teasing, but Jenny was hardly in a joking mood. Glancing at her rain-splotched uniform, she said, "This isn't a social call. And you know it."

He groaned as he whacked off a huge hunk from the roll of summer sausage. "Don't tell me you're here to write me up again."

"I'm here to tell you what a despicable swine you are!" She took a step toward him.

He turned and held up both arms in a gesture of surrender. "That weapon of yours isn't loaded, is it?"

Jenny looked pointedly at her revolver, then at him. "It would hardly be any good to me if it wasn't loaded," she retorted.

"Then I'm sorry. Whatever I've done, I'm sorry."

Her green eyes blazing, she quickly closed the distance between them. "You know what you've done. And you're not one bit sorry."

"If you're talking about the safety meeting, well—"

"Well, what? Do you go around getting back at every woman who turns you down?"

He shot her a wounded look. "I don't ever feel I *have* to get back at anyone. And what makes you think I have that many women turning me down?"

She rolled her eyes, and her breath came in short, angry spurts. "I have never encountered such arrogance in my life," she muttered, more to herself than to him.

Chuckling, he dropped his arms and reached behind him for the hunk of sausage. "And I've never seen a woman who riled as easily as you," he said, then held the food up to her lips. "Here, take a bite. I guarantee it'll soothe that redheaded temper of yours."

The man was crazy! Or was she, for thinking she could come here and put him in his place?

"I don't want to eat! I want to—"

"Kill me?" He bit off a piece of the spicy meat and began to chew with relish. "Okay, go ahead. My will is up to date. And there's not really anyone around who'll grieve over me that much, anyway. I only hate that I'll miss reading about it all in the papers. I wonder how it will read? Police Officer murders trucking mogul because he requested her to speak at safety meeting." Lucas shook his head. "I hate to tell you this, Jenny, but that motive sounds damn flimsy. Everyone will think we really had a lovers' quarrel and you shot me in a fit of passion."

"It's a tempting thought," she muttered.

He threw back his head and laughed. As Jenny watched him, she felt her fury drain away like muddy water. She couldn't stay angry with him. Not when he was being so affable, so completely amused by her fit of temper.

"Jenny, you're one of the most humorous women I've ever met."

She wasn't sure that was a compliment. "You think I'm funny? I'm not trying to be."

He chuckled again, then his expression sobered. He reached out and touched the wave of hair near her right eye.

"I know. That's why you are." His finger gently moved up and down the silky strand of hair. "I've never known a redhead, either. At least, not a redheaded woman. I thought that old saying about redheads and temper was just an old wives' tale. You've proved that wrong."

Jenny's breathing was suddenly shallow. So much so that she found it difficult to reply.

"I don't normally have a temper," she said. "I just don't like it when a man—" She drew in a deep breath, then let it out with relief as he pulled his hand away from her hair. "When a man tries to manipulate me," she finished.

Surprise swept over his features. "You think that's what I was trying to do when I talked to your captain about the safety meeting?"

"I certainly do."

His face suddenly stoic, he turned to the cutting board and a block of Colby cheese. "If you'll call my secretary, she'll confirm that I already had that safety meeting scheduled, but the person who was going to be there to speak had a family emergency and had to cancel. Naturally you came to mind as a replacement."

Naturally, Jenny repeated to herself. Then she remembered his story about the football game, and a thread of doubt wove its way into her thoughts. Maybe she had jumped the gun. Maybe, God help her, she was being presumptuous in thinking he'd go to that much trouble just to see her again.

"Is that really true?"

Doubt wavered in her voice, and something else, Lucas thought. Something that made her sound terribly vulnerable and utterly feminine. It got to him far more than anything she could have said.

Turning to her, he said, "It is true. And I'll go a step further and admit that asking you to speak at the meeting was my way of killing two birds with one stone. I wanted to see you again. And I also knew that you'd do a good job with the safety lecture."

She opened her mouth to speak, but he went on before she could put up any sort of protest.

"However, if you're so against talking to my men about safety, then I'll understand perfectly if you don't want to do it. I'll tell your captain that I had to cancel the meeting for some reason and that I won't be needing you."

Jenny couldn't believe what she was hearing. Yet he looked and sounded perfectly sincere. With a brief shake of her head, she asked, "You'd do that? For me?"

Doubt was still in her voice, and Lucas wondered why she found his gesture so hard to accept. Had she never had people change their plans simply to suit her wishes before?

"Of course I would. I wouldn't get any pleasure in forcing you to be there."

Why not? she wondered. Marcus had enjoyed forcing her to do his bidding. Why should this man be any different?

"That does seem like what you were trying to do," she said after a moment.

He smiled at her, then turned to the cheese. After he'd whittled off a hunk that equaled the size of the sausage, he tossed it onto a dessert plate. "Maybe I was. But only because I was afraid you'd turn down my invitation. Now you're going to turn it down anyway, aren't you?"

Without waiting for her to answer, he crossed to a large refrigerator, pulled out a jar of green olives and another of kosher pickles, then carried both to the counter.

As Jenny watched him spear the condiments onto the small plate, her mind whirled in total confusion. She'd come to Lucas Lowrimore's house to tell him he could take his safety meeting and jump off a cliff with it. But now she didn't know what she wanted!

"I didn't say that." Shaking her head, Jenny reached up and smoothed her hands over her rain-damp hair. The action caused the twisted bun at the back of her head to loosen. Before she could jam the hairpins in place, the red mass came tumbling down around her shoulders.

"Damn it!" she muttered.

Lucas glanced at her, then grinned at the sight of her hair. "I don't have a special requirement for hairstyles in my house. As far as I'm concerned you can leave it loose."

But Jenny didn't want it loose. Leaving her hair down would make it look as though she was getting relaxed and comfortable with him, and that was the very last thing she wanted him to think.

"I'm...still in uniform," she hastily replied as she twisted the thick curls into a bun and jabbed the hairpins securely in place.

"But you're not on duty," he reminded her.

The task with her hair done, she dropped her hands to her sides and drew back her shoulders to a stance of stiff attention. "I still have an image to uphold."

Lucas made a point of looking around the quiet room. "I only see you and me here. And I promise I won't tell anybody I saw your hair touch your collar."

"You're making fun of me now," she said, frowning at him.

He shook his head. "I'd never do that." Motioning for her to follow him, he carried two plates to a built-in booth situated by a large-paned window. "Come on, let's eat. I know you're hungry."

"I was hungry," she admitted, "until Captain Morgan ordered me to speak at your safety meeting."

He laughed. "Well, surely you've gotten your appetite back now. I've given you a reprieve. Besides, I've just made a fresh pot of coffee, and it's cold outside. A cup will warm you up."

Jenny hardly needed warming up. She was already as hot as blue blazes. Thanks to him!

But she couldn't admit such a thing to him, and anyway she needed a few more minutes to make up her mind about the safety meeting. He'd given her an out. Was she going to take it and feel guilty about shunning her job, or do the job and endure another meeting with this provocative man?

Reluctantly, she joined him at the booth and was immediately surprised to see that while he'd been whittling and whacking cheese and sausage, he'd made a plate for her, too.

After unbuckling her gun belt, she slid onto the vinyl seat and set the weapon safely beside her.

"Have you ever had to use that thing?" he asked, nodding toward her revolver.

She expected to find distaste on his face. Instead she saw simple curiosity. "I've had to draw it a few times. But I've never had to fire it. And I'm very proud of that."

"I'm sure you are." He reached for an insulated pitcher, then filled two thick cups with strong coffee. Pushing one of the cups over to her, he asked, "Cream or sugar?"

She shook her head. "I'm a plain Jane. It's easier that way."

Lucas wasn't quite sure if she was referring to the coffee or something else. In any case, he decided now wasn't the time to ask. She looked very uncomfortable, and he knew one wrong word would have her flying out of here as quickly as she had appeared.

"Does it offend you to see a woman carrying a gun?" she asked bluntly.

His brows peaked at her unexpected question. "No. Should it?"

A sweep of soft color stained her cheeks. "Most men find it intimidating."

Lucas wondered if she liked that idea. Was she the sort of woman who liked to have the upper hand over a man, even if it meant she had to carry a weapon to do it? No, he didn't think so. She didn't seem full of herself. And she was obviously very, very serious about her job.

He gave her a brief smile as he offered her a basket of assorted crackers. "I admire any person, man or woman, who works to protect the people."

"I think you really mean that."

He bit into a sliver of cheese. "I do. You sound surprised."

Everything, absolutely *everything* about him surprised Jenny. "We cops don't often get a vote of admiration."

Lucas watched her cradle the coffee cup with both hands as she brought it to her lips. Her hands were small, the nails clipped short and unvarnished. She had the ivory pink complexion of a redhead, which only made her green eyes stand out that much more. There was something about those eyes, he thought, that hinted at hidden passion and broken dreams. And suddenly he wanted to know everything there was to know about Jenny Prescott. He wanted to know her loves and losses, her wants and wishes, and more than anything he wanted to know what it would take to put a smile on her face. A smile just for him.

"Aside from the safety factor, hungry children get to eat Thanksgiving dinner and find a toy under the tree at Christmastime because of you and your fellow officers." He shook his head. "You may not feel appreciated, Jenny. But those little children thank you a thousand times over."

It was hard to stay vexed with a man who got a soft glow in his eyes just speaking the word *children*. She couldn't. And maybe he knew that. But for the moment she didn't care. Having a little snack with the man wasn't going to harm her. And it had been so long since she'd had a conversation with a man who wasn't a fellow officer.

Jenny picked up a round slice of summer sausage and squashed it between two crackers. "You really do like children, don't you?"

Smiling over the rim of his coffee cup, he said, "I love children."

"Have you ever wanted any of your own?" she asked, trying her best to make the question sound casual.

His expression grew serious. "While I was younger I never really thought about it. But these past few years... Well, I don't have any brothers or sisters or anybody. Maybe that's why—" He broke off as his eyes traveled slowly around the room. "I'm beginning to think I'd like to have a family of my own."

Lucas Lowrimore seemed like the last man to be the fatherly sort. He had the looks and the money to live a glamorous life-style. Did he honestly want to be a married man with children, or was he merely saying that because he thought it was the thing a woman wanted to hear?

Jenny, your cynicism is rearing its head again, she scolded herself. Lucas Lowrimore could be totally sincere. But then again, he might just be spouting words. Marcus had taught her to be very suspicious of men. Being a cop had taught her to be wary of people in general. If those lessons had made her a cynic, then she couldn't help it.

"That's hard to believe," she finally said.

He laughed. "It doesn't bother you to speak your mind, does it?"

She didn't smile. "I usually say what I think around a man. And I want him to do the same."

He cocked his head as he studied her face. "Hmm, well, if he always spoke his mind he might get into trouble."

A hint of a smile played around her mouth. "That depends on what's on his mind at the time."

Reaching for his coffee cup, he continued to study her. "You don't like men much, do you? Or is it just me you don't like?"

Suddenly Jenny laughed, and the unexpected sound caught Lucas totally off guard.

"You sound like my friend Savanna. She calls me a man-hater."

"Are you?"

She laughed again, although this time it was a tense, strained sound. "No. And I'm not a man hunter, either." She lifted her eyes to his and held them there. "The roses you sent me were very beautiful, and I'll keep them until they wilt. But please don't send me anymore. You'd only be wasting your money."

How sad, Lucas thought, that she considered herself unworthy of flowers. "If you get enjoyment from them, then my money wasn't wasted."

Jenny's eyes fell to her plate. For not the first time tonight, his selfless attitude took her aback.

"Well, I—" She broke off, furious with herself because she couldn't make her heart quit pounding. Nor could she make herself look at him. "What I meant was . . . I'm not interested in romance. Short- or long-term."

Seconds passed and he didn't make a reply. Jenny lifted her eyes to his and was surprised to see an amused look on his face.

"Are you always so serious, Jenny Prescott?"

No, normally she didn't have trouble with a pounding heart or fits of emotions. Normally, she would have never dreamed of going to a man's house and confronting him about a bouquet of roses! But then she hadn't quite been herself since she and Orville had stopped Lucas on the street and she'd watched him climb arrogantly out of his black sports car.

"It pays to be serious, Lucas," she said, then with a burst of frustration, she bit into the crackers and sausage.

He liked the way she said his name with authority. She had a deep, rich voice full of strength and character. Lucas had often been told by acquaintances in Texas that his mother was a weak woman, and because of her weakness she'd lost her life. Lucas had only been two at the time she'd died, and even though he'd been too young to know her, he wondered if that was the reason he'd searched so hard to find a strong woman for himself, a woman who could stand up to him or anything life had to throw at her. Up until now, his search had been fruitless. But that had changed the moment Jenny Prescott had slapped a ticket into his palm.

"How long have you been on the police force?" he asked.

She relaxed a bit. This was something she could talk about without feeling concerned. "Ten years."

"That's a long time for someone so young."

"It's a long time for anybody."

Her frankness made him curve his lips in a faint grin. "What made you decide to be a policewoman? Was your dad on the force or something?"

Jenny wanted to snort, but stopped herself just short of emitting the cynical sound. "I wouldn't know. My father left my mother and me long before I was born," she said, her voice a little caustic.

"I'm sorry."

Jenny shrugged. "Don't be. I can't miss what I've never known." She pushed an olive across her plate, then stabbed it with a fork. "As for wanting to be a policewoman, I thought I'd look good in blue."

Behind her flip words, Lucas heard something entirely different. She was a woman with a lot of pride. Pride that she wouldn't sacrifice for anyone or anything.

"You're pulling my leg now."

A brief smile touched her lips. "Yes. I would have been a policewoman no matter the color of the uniform. Because I wanted to help people. To make a difference." She looked at him, then laughed under her breath. "Corny, huh? I sound like a damn recruiter."

His dark eyes combed her face, cherished its soft, regal beauty. "I think it sounds nice. I think you're nice, Jenny. Even though you want me to think you're not."

Jenny reached for her gun belt and carefully strapped it around her. She had to get out of here. Lucas was saying things to her she didn't want to hear, things she hadn't heard in years that reminded her how lonely her life really was.

"Well, thanks for the snack, Lucas. But I've got to get home."

Before he could say anything she slid from the booth. "I'll do your safety meeting," she told him. "Only because I think it's important to educate drivers. Not because—"

"Of me," Lucas finished for her. Easing to his feet, he stood looking at her. "Yes, I know what you're trying to tell me. There are no strings to be attached. You're not in the market for romance. Long- or short-term. You're not a man-hater, nor are you a man hunter. You like roses, but don't want a man to send them to you. Have I gotten everything right so far?"

He smiled at her, and just for a moment Jenny felt a part of her weaken. He was so good to look at, so strong and vibrant and masculine. If she was a brave woman, she would be tempted to get closer to him. She might even be inclined to touch him, kiss him, discover for herself if being in his arms would be as good as she imagined it might be. But Jenny wasn't a brave woman. She only pretended to be. And right now Lucas Lowrimore was scaring her to death.

She'd come here in a fit of temper, determined to tell him that it would be a cold day in July before she'd set foot near L.L. Freight Company. Instead, she'd wound up eating his food and promising to speak at his damned safety meeting.

"So it seems," she said, more to herself than to him, then quickly started out of the kitchen.

Lucas walked beside her, gently touching the small of her back as he guided her through the darkened rooms until the two of them eventually reached the front entrance of the house.

At the door, Lucas gently took her hand in his and Jenny quivered like a snared rabbit.

"I'm really glad you came to see me tonight, Jenny. I've enjoyed your company."

She hadn't come to please him or give him company. But in spite of herself, she'd ended up doing both. And that made her feel extremely foolish.

"I'm sure you never lack company," she said, withdrawing her hand and quickly stepping away from him.

She was right. He had more than his share of friends and business people stopping by the house. But none of those people were anything like Jenny. She was in a category all by herself.

"You might be surprised about that, Jenny," he said softly.

She took another step backward and immediately the doorknob jabbed her in the middle of the spine. Jenny twisted around and grabbed for the brass knob as though it was a line to freedom. Once she was outside on the small enclosed porch, she let out a relieved breath.

"Well, I'll see you at the meeting then," she said, as she turned to start down the steps toward her car.

Suddenly Lucas's hand shot out and grabbed her arm. Jenny's head whipped around and she stared at him with wide, dark eyes.

"What are you doing?"

Her voice was sharp and full of warning. It took Lucas by such surprise that he immediately dropped his hold on her.

"I'm..." His words trailed away as his eyes roamed her face in the darkness. She was afraid of him. The idea hit him like a knife in the heart. "I just wanted to tell you how much I appreciate you agreeing to do the safety meeting. It means a lot to me. And it will to my drivers, too."

Jenny quickly looked away from him and blinked at the hot moisture burning the back of her eyes. She felt like an idiot and knew he was probably labeling her as something even worse. It had been a long time, years, in fact, since she'd reacted so defensively to the touch of a man.

But then it had been years since a man had made her heart beat fast, made her think of herself as a woman and caused her guard to momentarily slip like it had tonight.

Glancing at him, she said, "You're welcome, Lucas."

He stepped closer and took her hand. The moment his fingers curled around hers, he realized he'd never in his life felt such a need to comfort and reassure. He wanted to take her face between his hands, kiss the quiver from her lips and tell her she had nothing to fear from him.

But words were oftentimes easily spoken, and he had the feeling that Jenny Prescott would need more than words to gain his trust. He'd have to earn it.

"Friends?" he asked softly.

She could never be a friend to this man, or anything more, Jenny thought resignedly. But for tonight it was easier to let him think they were friends.

Nodding, she slipped her hand from his and sprinted down the steps and out to her car.

As Lucas watched her drive away he realized that behind that badge of courage she wore pinned to her breast was a vulnerable woman, a woman who needed him. She didn't know that yet. But sooner or later she would. He was going to make sure of it.

As for her being a cop, well, Lucas didn't want to think about that problem right now.

Chapter Four

The next morning, Jenny sat at the small dining table in her apartment and methodically went down a checklist of subjects she wanted to include in her safety lecture. Many of them were simple, commonsense driving skills and general safety precautions. If Lucas was expecting something more high-tech from her presentation, he was going to be disappointed.

With an exasperated sigh, Jenny set the list to one side and rubbed her fingers across the furrows in her forehead. Darn it, she didn't care what Lucas Lowrimore thought. It had been wrong of him to coerce her into his safety meeting thing, anyway.

But he hadn't really coerced her, she reluctantly reminded herself. He had given her an easy out. She'd just been too spineless, too momentarily charmed by the man to say no.

A knock at the door interrupted Jenny's dour thoughts.

She went to answer it and found her friend Savanna standing in the hallway.

"Come in, honey! What are you doing out so early this morning?"

With one hand clutched against her midsection, the petite blonde quickly stepped into the apartment. "I can't— talk now!"

Seeing the greenish white pallor on her friend's face, Jenny instantly grabbed Savanna's elbow and steered her toward the bathroom. "Go."

A few minutes later, Savanna emerged from the bathroom with rosy cheeks and a weak smile on her face.

"Feeling better?" Jenny asked. She patted the couch cushion next to her. "Come here. I fixed you a ginger ale and found a couple of saltines, too."

Savanna sank gratefully onto the striped couch and reached for the cool drink on a low coffee table. "Thanks, Jen. I'm much better now. In fact, I wasn't a bit sick until I ran into the janitor several doors back. The floor cleaner he was using smelled like dead rats. Ugh!"

"I can't imagine being nauseated every day for nearly four months," Jenny said with a shake of her head. "And you still manage to keep smiling."

Savanna laughed, then sipped the ginger ale. "And eating." Seemingly revived, she jumped to her feet, lifted the hem of her blouse and patted her slightly rounded tummy. "Look at this. Growing, don't you think?"

"I've seen grapefruits bigger than that," Jenny teased.

Savanna waved away her words and sank onto the couch. "Well, I don't care what you say, I feel fat." She smiled and sighed. "But Joe says I look beautiful."

"You do. And of course Joe says you look beautiful pregnant. The man is crazy about you."

The dreamy glow on Savanna's face said she knew her husband loved her. For not the first time, Jenny looked at her friend and wondered about her own life.

It was too late for her to find the same sort of happiness she could see on Savanna's face. Oh, maybe not physically too late, she thought wistfully. She was certainly still young and fit enough to bear children. But emotionally her heart was just too old, too scarred and used up to ever try to love again.

"The reason I'm out early this morning, I thought you might go shopping with me. I'm going to surprise Megan with a few new things to wear to school. And then I thought we might make a trip to the beauty salon. My treat."

Still in a thin cotton housecoat, Jenny turned toward her friend. "I could certainly use the trip to the salon. And I'd love to go. But—"

"Don't tell me you have to work," Savanna said with a groan. "I thought your shift didn't start until late this evening?"

Jenny shook her head. "I'm on a separate assignment from Orville today. I'm giving a safety lecture at a local trucking firm. You've probably seen some of the semis on the interstate. The ones with the big red L.L. Freight written on them?"

Savanna nodded. "Yes, I know the trucks. In fact, I know where the trucking yard is. That's a big place, Jenny. How many drivers will you be speaking to?"

Jenny lifted one shoulder and let it fall. She hadn't been thinking about how many men would be in the audience. She'd been thinking about *one* man. And she'd been wondering what it was going to be like to see him again.

"I'm not sure. It doesn't really matter. The lecture would be the same whether the audience was five or fifty."

"I don't recall you ever doing anything like this before," Savanna said with a curious glance at Jenny. "Is this something new for you?"

Jenny shook her head. "No. I've done them before. Although it's been a long time."

"Well, all I can say is I'm glad it's you and not me. I'm terrible at public speaking. I think my high school speech teacher gave me a passing grade just to get me out of her hair."

"Actually," Jenny said, rising restlessly to her feet, "I'm not fond of these things myself. But when Captain Morgan says do it, I'm in no position to argue. Although in this case I . . ."

"You what?"

Jenny glanced at her friend as she tried to decide how much to tell her. In the end, the need to confide in someone won out. "I wanted to argue loudly."

Savanna crossed her legs and patted the seat Jenny had just vacated. "Somehow I get the feeling you're holding out on me. Sit down and tell me what's going on. Are you having trouble with your job?"

Jenny made a sound that could only be described as strangled laughter. "I'm having—" Easing down on the couch, she shook her head at Savanna. "Don't laugh. But I'm having trouble with a man."

Savanna stared, dumbfounded. "Man trouble? You? What sort of trouble could you be having with a man? I've never seen you look at one twice. Have you been—" Her eyes suddenly wide, Savanna stopped and leaned toward Jenny. "Are you seeing a man, Jenny?"

"No!"

The word rushed out quickly. Too quickly, in fact, because Savanna was suddenly studying her with a sly gleam in her eye.

"You have! I know it. I can tell you're lying."

Jenny let out a resigned sigh. "Honestly, Savanna, I haven't been seeing a man in the way you're thinking. Although I have gotten myself sort of—tangled up with one."

"What do you mean, tangled up? Like in entwined limbs?"

"No! Nothing like that!"

Frowning, Jenny jumped to her feet and crossed to the dining table. Without realizing what she was doing, she stacked several papers together, squared their corners, then tossed them on the tabletop.

"Jenny—"

"Orville and I made a traffic stop the other evening," she blurted out before Savanna had the chance to go any further.

The blonde smiled. "That's big news, Jen."

"Quit being smart-mouthed and listen," Jenny told her as she walked across the room toward her. "The driver was Lucas T. Lowrimore. The man that owns L.L. Freight Company."

"Oh," Savanna said slowly, "is that why you're doing the safety meeting there?"

Jenny's full lips twisted. "In a way."

"Jen, you're being evasive. Did you get into trouble with your captain because you gave one of the city's big businessmen a ticket?"

"No. Quite the contrary," she told her, then with a resigned sigh, she sat beside Savanna. "I'm not having trouble with Captain Morgan. It's Lucas Lowrimore. He's—he's been pursuing me. Sort of," she added quickly as she watched Savanna's mouth form a surprised O.

"Pursuing you? Really? What's the man like?"

"He's tall, dark, rich and sexy."

"In that order?"

Jenny couldn't help smiling at Savanna's question. "No. Sexy is the prominent word here."

"Ooh, now we're getting somewhere," Savanna said. Sipping her ginger ale, she scooted to a more comfortable position on the couch. "Tell me all about him."

"Savanna," Jenny scolded, "there's nothing to tell. I mean not anything like you think. The man simply wanted me to go out with him. And I refused."

"Oh, but Jenny, why? This might be the one true one. The one good man I know is out there looking for you, wanting to love you."

Jenny snorted. Once she might have believed and hoped there was someone out there for her. But life with Marcus had taught her that romantic notions were foolish, risky things.

"There isn't such a man, Savanna. At least not for me."

"Only because you don't want one."

"You're darn right I don't want one. I'm doing just fine like I am. I don't have to answer to anyone. I don't have to be afraid or humiliated or—oh, you know how I feel about this, Savanna. There's no need to talk about Lucas. I'm not about to get involved with him. Even if he thinks otherwise."

A smug smile played on Savanna's lips. "Sounds like you're already involved. You just called him Lucas."

"I call Orville *Orville,* too. But that doesn't mean I'm crazy about the guy."

Savanna let out a knowing laugh. "You're so transparent, Jenny. I can see your eyes crackling fire just at the mention of this man's name. And I couldn't be happier about it."

Jenny reached for the ginger ale in Savanna's hand. "I think you better let me have this. I'm the one getting sick now."

Savanna handed the drink to her friend. "So are you going to be seeing him today at the lecture you're giving?"

"I hope not."

"Why? Afraid you might be tempted?"

Jenny grimaced. "Yes."

Savanna reached over and patted Jenny's knee. "Take my advice, Jen, give in and say yes. You might find out you like the man."

That was just it, Jenny thought glumly. She already knew she liked Lucas. She didn't want to. But she did. And that only strengthened her resolve to keep her distance from the man. If she didn't, she might be foolish enough to let that liking turn into loving.

"Forget it, Savanna," she said after a moment. "Just because you're happily married and blissfully in love doesn't mean I can be, too."

With a knowing little smile, Savanna plucked the glass of ginger ale from Jenny's fingers. "We'll see, dear friend. We'll see."

Later that afternoon, Jenny entered the office building of L.L. Freight Company. A young woman seated at a desk in the foyer directed her up to the third floor, where Lucas's private office was located.

Rather than take the elevator, Jenny climbed the stairs, then walked down the corridor in search of a door marked with Lucas's name. Once she found it, she knocked lightly.

As Jenny waited for an answer, she discovered her palms were wet. With a disgusted groan she rubbed them together and took two deep breaths. Darn it, she wasn't a nervous person. As a policewoman she'd faced all sorts of situations, some of them life threatening. So why was the idea of seeing Lucas Lowrimore again turning her inside out?

The door suddenly opened, and Jenny found herself looking at an older woman dressed in a hot pink suit and matching spiked high heels. She was peering at Jenny over a pair of outrageous rhinestone-studded reading glasses.

"Oh, there you are," she said, a bright smile on her face. "You must be Officer Prescott. Please come in."

Jenny followed the secretary into a spacious work area furnished with a desk, file chests, couch and several armchairs.

"I'm Lilah," the woman said as she offered her hand to Jenny. "I'm sure Mr. Lowrimore has told you all about me. And if he hasn't, he should have."

Jenny shook Lilah's hand "Actually, Lucas hasn't said—"

"Oh, you don't have to worry about being subtle around me, honey. Mr. Lowrimore always tells me exactly what he thinks. Just like these beads I'm wearing today." Lilah fingered the purple-hued pearls wrapped choker style around her neck. "He says these look gaudy with this pink suit I'm wearing. But I told him he doesn't know anything about fashion. A woman has to make a statement about herself. Especially if she wants to be noticed. Don't you think so, Miss Prescott?"

"Please call me Jenny."

Still smiling, Lilah took Jenny by the elbow and led her to the couch situated a few steps away from an inner door.

"Have a seat, honey. I just talked to Velma, our dispatcher, a moment ago. She says the drivers won't all be back in the yard for a while yet. Besides, Mr. Lowrimore won't care if you start right on the button. Would you like a cup of coffee? I just made a fresh pot in his office. It won't take a moment to get it."

Jenny hadn't come here to sit and drink coffee. But she could hardly start the meeting until all the truckers arrived. Taking a seat on the couch, she said, "I'm fine. Please don't bother Mr. Lowrimore."

Lilah waved a dismissive hand at her. "Oh, don't worry about bothering Mr. Lowrimore. He's not here." She clucked her tongue in disapproval. "He was called out unexpectedly to that downtown shelter of his. His electrical contractor was having some sort of problem with the city fire code or something. I tell you, that man just takes on too much."

So Lucas wasn't here, Jenny thought as the secretary disappeared into his office. The news should have had her sighing with relief. But to her dismay she felt deflated. All week she'd been thinking about the things he might say to her, the way he would look at her and the way she might feel when she looked at him. She'd anticipated this day with every fiber of her being. She'd equally dreaded it. And now Lucas wasn't even here, and a part of her had wilted. She couldn't understand it.

"Here you go," Lilah said as she returned. "I left it black. I had a feeling you drank it that way."

Jenny took the foam cup from her. "Thank you, I do."

Rather than going to her desk, Lilah perched a hip on the arm of the couch a short distance from Jenny. An exotic floral perfume floated around her, and though the woman was outrageously flamboyant, she made a part of Jenny wish she was wearing a dress instead of a uniform.

"I've never known a policewoman before," Lilah said. "I never expected you to be so beautiful. But then I should have known you would be. Mr. Lowrimore never lies about things like that." She laughed and waved a jeweled hand at Jenny. "Mr. Lowrimore never lies about anything. But I figure you already knew that about him."

Lucas had told this woman she was beautiful? Jenny didn't know what to think. "Actually I don't really know Lucas that well. Have you worked for him long?"

"Since he started this business. And from that day he's been the most kind, generous boss I've ever had. You see, Mr. Lowrimore and I go way back. I use to work for a lawyer. He came in one day to get some legal advice, and while he was waiting for his appointment, the two of us got to visiting about one thing and another. He told me all about the business venture he had in mind and asked me if I'd like to come to work for him. I took an instant liking to him. So I said yes."

"Just like that?" Jenny was amazed. Even though Lilah appeared to be a little bit offbeat, she knew the woman had to be a competent secretary or Lucas wouldn't have kept her on for so long. Still, Jenny couldn't imagine any woman doing such an impulsive thing. "You didn't really know him, or if the business would survive."

Lilah laughed softly. "All it took for me was one good look at Mr. Lowrimore. He's not a man who's going to fail at anything he goes to do. You know what I mean?"

Jenny knew exactly what the woman meant. And it made her wonder how she could stand up to him if he really tried to pursue a relationship with her. "He's certainly appeared to make a success out of trucking," she said as she glanced around the plush office.

"Mr. Lowrimore worked himself to the bone in those early years. 'Course, he could coast now if he wanted to. But those children of his take up a lot of his time. I tell him he needs to get married and have a few of his own. A man with a heart like his—well, it's just a sin for him not to be a father. But Lucas has ideas of his own about that."

Before Jenny could reply, the telephone rang. Lilah went to answer it. Their conversation ended, Jenny walked to the plate-glass windows lining the opposite wall. As she sipped her coffee, she watched several eighteen-wheelers roll into the huge yard below.

Even though Orville had insisted Lucas was a wealthy man, she'd never expected L.L. Freight Company to be this big. How had one man turned so little into so much? she wondered. Why hadn't a woman been around to share it with him? And those children Lilah spoke of, were those the ones she'd seen him with in the park?

Stop it, Jenny, she scolded herself. *You don't need to know anything more about Lucas Lowrimore's life. The less you think about him the better off you'll be.*

Lilah's voice suddenly sounded behind her. Jenny glanced over her shoulder to see the woman rising from her desk. "Velma just called up from the yard. She says the last truck has made it back. If you're ready, I'll take you down to the meeting room and help you set up."

Jenny turned from the window and tossed the remains of her coffee into a trash basket. The time had arrived to get this lecture over with and put Lucas Lowrimore out of her mind once and for all.

By the time Jenny started the safety meeting, the room was packed with men. She started off with simple, basic rules of good, defensive driving, then went on to other things, like how inertia affected big rigs, particularly tankers, as they made sharp turns. She pointed out how to safely mark the highway with hazard blocks when a truck was stalled on the side, and what to do when a truck accidently spilled chemical or flammable contents. She discussed weights, speeds and braking time in feet and seconds. The list Jenny went through was long, and covered the gamut of roadway safety.

An hour later she was relieved to see the men were still listening attentively as she wound up her program.

"In closing, men, just remember that fifty-five does save lives, and I wish each of you safe and happy driving. Now if someone will get the lights, I'll let you all get back to work. Thank you all."

The lights went on and the men politely applauded. Jenny looked over the audience to nod her appreciation. As she did, she spotted one lone figure leaning casually against the wall at the back of the room.

Lucas! Dear Lord, how long had he been there?

He began to walk toward her. Unable to do anything else, Jenny watched him until several of the drivers came up to shake her hand and tell her how much they enjoyed her talk. With her attention momentarily diverted from Lucas, she was able to calm her pounding heart and tell herself she wasn't really glad to see the man. Even so, she could feel a bright flush on her cheeks, and for some odd reason she kept getting the urge to smile.

Eventually the truck drivers cleared the room. Lucas, who'd been standing to one side, joined her at the utility table she'd used to set up her projector.

"I was right about you," he said. "I knew you'd get to my men."

The sound of his voice sent shivers of pleasure through Jenny. Desperately trying to ignore her reaction to his nearness, she looked at him. "How long were you standing back there?"

A lopsided smile curved his mouth. Jenny wanted to let out a loud, helpless groan. He might not be a traditionally handsome man, but he was far too sexy for her peace of mind.

"Oh, I came in shortly after you started. Why? You wouldn't have changed your program because of me, would you?"

Judging by the lazy, daunting way he asked the question, Lucas already knew he'd distracted her. And that made her far more angry at herself than at him.

"No. I wasn't doing it for you," she told him, her voice cool.

A smile on his face, he said, "I'm glad. Because for once I can say the men enjoyed a safety meeting. You did a great job, Jenny."

Just when she was about to decide she didn't really like the man, he turned around and complimented her, she thought wryly. Or was it just flattery, a tactic on his part to soften her? She hated to think so. But doubting a man's motives was second nature to Jenny. She hated being so cynical and suspicious all the time, but Marcus had left deep scars inside her. She couldn't simply trust Lucas because his friends and employees said he was a nice, generous man.

"I'm sure they've heard it all a hundred times before."

"They have. That's why I needed you to make them sit up and take notice."

"I was only doing my job."

"And doing it well," he added softly.

His dark gaze was roaming her face, touching it as though he was glad to finally be seeing it again. Jenny wondered if these past few days he'd been thinking about her the way she'd been thinking about him.

Giving herself a hard mental slap, Jenny turned her attention to the slides scattered across the tabletop. "I—I'd better get these things gathered up and back to the station house."

She began scooping up the slides and placing them in a small metal box. Without waiting to be asked, Lucas went to the portable screen and scrolled it back into its cylinder.

"I hope Lilah assisted you with all this," he said as he worked. "I had planned on being here to help, but unfortunately I was called out at the last minute."

To a shelter, Lilah had told her. Jenny found herself wanting to ask more, but she quickly bit her tongue. As long as Lucas wasn't breaking the law, it was none of her business where he went or what he'd been doing.

"Lilah was very helpful," Jenny assured him. She closed the lid on the projector, then glanced quickly around the utility table. "Well, it looks like that's everything. I guess I'll take this stuff down to the car and be on my way."

It didn't surprise Lucas to see Jenny so eager to leave. From the moment he'd first walked over to her, she'd tightened up like a slingshot ready to be fired. If she'd been any other woman sending him such negative signals, Lucas would have politely said thank you for the lecture and goodbye. But Jenny wasn't just any woman. She was a woman he wanted to know. Inside and out. Maybe he was a fool, just asking to be hurt by setting his sights on a woman cop. Hell, he was being more than a fool. He was being downright crazy. But even knowing all this, he couldn't seem to stop wanting her.

"I'll help you," he said and quickly reached for the projector case.

Jenny shook her head. "There's no need. I think I can manage it all in one trip."

The smile he gave her said she wasn't about to get rid of him that easily. "Nonsense. Besides, I haven't had much exercise today. If you don't let me carry this down for you, then I won't have an excuse to take the stairs up to my office."

The last thing Jenny wanted to do was appear ungrateful, so she picked up her briefcase and started out of the room. "Oh, well, I surely wouldn't want to be the cause of you missing your exercise."

Grinning, Lucas grabbed the screen and followed her out the door. On the ride down in the elevator, Jenny remained silent, her eyes on the door. Lucas stood quietly beside her, his gaze discreetly venturing over her curves beneath the blue uniform.

His thoughts had been on this woman all week. In fact, little else had been on his mind. And during all his thinking, Lucas had kept telling himself Jenny wasn't the strong woman he'd been searching for. She wasn't the woman he wanted to bear his children, to grow old and gray with. She wasn't the woman he wanted as a wife. Several times he had promised himself that once this meeting was over today, he would never make the effort to see her again. But looking at her now, all soft and feminine inside those no-nonsense masculine clothes, he realized he wasn't the man of iron will he thought he was.

Outside the building the sky had become overcast and a cold wind was clipping briskly from the north. Jenny shivered in response as she unlocked the trunk of the patrol car and waited for Lucas to load the screen and projector.

"I want to thank you again for doing this, Jenny," he said as he shut the trunk. "It means a lot to me that you went to all this trouble."

She wished he didn't sound so sincere. And she wished to heaven he would quit thanking her. If he kept this up, she might start believing him.

Wrapping her arms around her to ward off the chill of the wind, Jenny glanced at him. "It wasn't any trouble. Captain Morgan gave me the rest of the afternoon off. So I'm having an easy shift today."

"I'm glad to hear that. Maybe you'll consider coming back soon to speak to the other half of my drivers?"

Her mouth formed an O. Taking it as a sign of indignation, Lucas quickly held up his hand. "I mean, only if you'd like to come back and speak to them. I certainly won't go over your head and speak to your captain about it. Promise."

He placed his hand on his chest, and suddenly Jenny couldn't help but smile at the gesture. At least for the time being, Lucas seemed to know he couldn't manipulate her. Just knowing that made Jenny relax a bit.

"I can't believe I was speaking to only half your drivers, Lucas. That was a large group of men in there today."

Jenny couldn't help but notice there was a certain amount of pride in the smile he gave her.

"L.L. Freight does employ a large number of truck drivers. You saw only half of them because I couldn't afford to shut them all down at once. We ship freight from coast to coast, and a lot of people are depending on us to be there at a promised time. I don't want anyone to miss having their Sunday roast or that new set of tires they ordered because we weren't there to haul it to them."

The wind was playing with his dark hair and the collar of his gray striped shirt. He was dressed in jeans rather than a suit today, and seeing him like this made it a little easier for Jenny to imagine him driving a big rig down the interstate. Still, he had come a long way since that time. But then so had she, she mused. Instead of a battered wife, she was a confident policewoman. And she'd never go back. Not for anyone. Not even for this man.

Releasing a breath she hadn't even known she was holding, she said, "Well, I'd better be going."

She walked to the driver's door. Lucas followed.

"Let me take you out to supper," he said suddenly.

Jenny had been about to slide beneath the steering wheel, but slowly turned her head to look at him.

"Lucas, you know how I—"

He held up one hand to ward off her protest. "Yes. I know how you feel about dating and men and all the rest of it. I haven't forgotten our little talk. I just wanted to repay you for giving the safety lecture."

Her eyes roamed his face, searching for what, she didn't know. But as she looked at him, she felt her resistance crumble like sandstone. "The city pays me. It would be illegal for you to give me any sort of pay or gifts."

"What about giving you plain old nourishment? From one friend to another?"

He was smiling again. Jenny decided it was no wonder Lilah had given up a secure job to follow this man into a risky business venture all those years ago. The man was persuasive. Not to mention lethally charming.

"One friend to another, huh?" She slid behind the wheel and stabbed the key into the ignition. Looking at him she said, "Put like that, I can hardly say no."

Lucas had been so ready for a cool refusal, he could hardly believe his ears. "You'll go?"

Jenny could see that she'd surprised him. Well, that hardly compared to what she'd done to herself. At the moment she felt completely shell-shocked. "Against my better judgment."

His dark eyes suddenly softened, and for one wild moment Jenny thought he was going to lean down and kiss her.

"I'll be by to pick you up at 6:30," he said. "What's your address?"

Feeling oddly light-headed, she gave it to him, then started the engine. "I'll be ready," she told him.

Who was she kidding? she asked herself a moment later as she backed out onto the street. She'd never be ready to spend more than fifteen minutes at a time with Lucas Lowrimore. God help her, how was she going to get through a whole dinner date with him?

Chapter Five

Jenny stood in front of the bathroom vanity cursing herself as she yanked the hairbrush through her long red curls. She really had lost her mind. It had been six years since she'd rid her life of Marcus. And since that time she'd been perfectly happy without a man. She hadn't had dates. But then she hadn't had heartaches, either. So what was she doing agreeing to go out with Lucas? Just asking to put herself through hell again?

She didn't really want to go out with Lucas! She just hadn't known how to say no without making an issue out of it.

Quit lying to yourself, a voice inside her mocked. *You know you're thrilled to be going out with the man. You're just too scared and stubborn to admit it.*

"Darn right, I'm scared," Jenny muttered.

Tossing down the hairbrush, she used her fingers to tuck her hair behind her left ear then secure it with a rhinestone-studded bobby pin. Just to add a little sparkle to her plain black dress, she told herself. She certainly wasn't doing anything extra to her appearance to impress Lucas.

In the living room, she stuffed a hanky and a tube of lipstick into her purse, then crossed to the kitchen. Maybe she should take a packet of antacids with her? The way her stomach was already tied into hard knots, she could hardly expect it to digest anything.

Before she could decide about the antacids, the doorbell rang. Hating the way her heart was suddenly beating in her throat, Jenny went to answer it.

After securing the chain latch, she cautiously opened the door wide enough to see Lucas standing on the other side. She opened the door the rest of the way.

"Good evening, Jenny. Ready to go?"

"Come in while I get my purse and coat," she invited.

Hardly able to look at anything but her, Lucas followed her into the small apartment. Up until now, he'd only imagined what her legs looked like. Now he could see them for himself, and the sight was far from disappointing.

She bent and picked up her purse from a low coffee table. Lucas cleared his throat, then ran a finger between his neck and shirt collar. "You'd better get a heavy coat. The weather has taken a turn for the worse. It was raining a few moments ago when I parked the car."

"I'll be right back," she told him, then quickly headed to the bedroom.

While she was gone, Lucas glanced around the room. It was small, but neat. Cozy, but not stifling. It was just the sort of place he'd imagined she might live in, and he wondered if she ever got lonely inside these walls. She'd said she would never dream of having a husband, but Lucas couldn't help but wonder if she ever longed for someone to love, someone to have children with.

Jenny returned from the bedroom. As she walked toward Lucas, she decided her apartment had never seemed so tiny and she'd never felt such a sudden need for oxygen.

"Maybe we'll get snow before the night is over," she said.

A red woolen coat was tossed over her arm. Lucas quickly helped her into it. Jenny's breath caught in her throat as he lifted her long hair from beneath the collar, then allowed it to gently cascade against her back.

His hands pausing on her shoulders, he said, "I love the snow. But if the roads become hazardous I worry about my drivers."

Heat from his body radiated out to her, and for a moment Jenny felt too weak to take one step away from him, much less walk to the door.

"Maybe I won't have to worry as much now," he went on, his voice close to her ear. "Since you lectured them about icy driving conditions."

"I hope they listened and learned," she said, her voice husky.

"I did."

Clearing her throat, Jenny summoned herself to move away from him. "Shall we go? I'm starving."

The restaurant Lucas had chosen was quietly elegant but not so ritzy that Jenny felt uncomfortable. He had shrimp, while she ate lamb. By the time they were having coffee and chocolate mousse for dessert, Jenny decided she'd been an idiot for being so nervous about this date.

There wasn't anything dangerous about having dinner with Lucas. She was thirty-four years old. She knew how men worked their wiles. She knew all their lines. All their tactics. She knew how not to fall for any of them. And she definitely knew not to fall in love. So what could she possibly have to worry about? she asked herself.

"Would you like something else?" Lucas asked as the waiter returned to fill their coffee cups.

Jenny shook her head. "Thank you, it was all very delicious, but I couldn't eat another bite."

"Nothing else for me, either," he told the waiter. "You can bring the check now."

While they waited for the young man to return with the bill, Lucas glanced at his watch. "I hope you don't have to be home just yet. There's a place not too far from here I'd like you to see."

The warm, relaxed glow surrounding Jenny suddenly vanished. She looked at him, her brows arched skeptically, her radar system on alert.

"Really?"

"Don't look at me like that," he said with a little chuckle. "I didn't siphon the gas tank down to a half gallon. I'll get you home safe and sound at a reasonable hour."

Maybe Lucas wasn't planning a seduction scene, but she still didn't think it would be wise to encourage him. "I'm really not a dancer, Lucas. And as for the movies, the only ones I like are the oldies."

He went around and helped her from her seat. "We're not going dancing or to the movies. Just for a little drive."

Jenny didn't argue further. She didn't want to spoil the evening. It had been ages since she'd been to a nice restaurant and had someone other than a fellow cop to talk to. Not that she and Lucas had discussed anything personal. So far they'd talked about the weather, politics and economics. But compared to vice and homicide those topics had been a breath of fresh air to Jenny.

Once they left the eating place and climbed into Lucas's black sports car, he headed south toward the interstate. Jenny left her coat on until the car heater made the interior comfortable, then she shrugged out of the arms and left it draped against the back of the seat.

The car was small, with only a narrow console separating the two of them. Lucas found his senses overwhelmed by the sight and scent of her. If he could do what he'd really like to do, he'd simply pull the car to the side of the street and haul her into his arms. She was a woman who was made for loving. From the passionate red flames of her hair down to slim graceful arch of her feet.

But Lucas knew if he were to act on his desire, he would never see Jenny Prescott again. Whether that might be good or bad for him, he didn't know. He only knew he wasn't about to take the chance of finding out. For once in his life, he was going to move slowly.

"You look very beautiful tonight, Jenny."

The two of them had been mostly quiet since they'd left the restaurant. Surprise and something like weariness was mirrored on Jenny's face as she slowly turned her head to look at him.

"You didn't need to say that, Lucas. I'm not about to jump out of the car or order you to take me home."

He frowned as he downshifted, then braked behind a slower moving vehicle.

"Jenny, has anyone ever told you you're jaded?"

He sounded a bit angry. No, not angry, she corrected herself. More like hurt. And suddenly she felt awful.

Sighing, she turned her head and looked out the window at the far-reaching lights of Oklahoma City. "I'm sorry, Lucas. I guess I sound like a hardened old woman to you. But you see, it's been a long time since I've been out with a man. And longer still since one told me I look beautiful. I guess—'' She paused and her chest hurt as she drew in a long breath. "I guess I don't know how to be with a man anymore."

Lucas had never heard such a lost sound in anyone's voice. Not even the homeless and orphaned children he dealt with. It made him wonder how Jenny had ever gotten to this point in her life. What had caused her to become so cynical?

He had to know. He wouldn't rest until he did.

"Don't worry about it, Jenny." Reaching over, he lifted her hand from her lap and clasped it in his.

Jenny looked at him, and suddenly without warning tears were burning the back of her eyes. He wasn't putting on a seductive act. He was simply being Lucas, a nice man. But she'd been too hard-nosed, too cautious and afraid to simply enjoy his company. Dear God, until this very moment she hadn't realized what she'd let herself become. And it frightened her.

"You might be surprised to learn that it's been a long time since I've told a woman she's beautiful." He grinned and squeezed her hand. "A guy has to have inspiration before he can say something like that."

Her fingers curled around his and clung tightly. "Thank you for not being offended, Lucas."

Lucas glanced away from the traffic and at Jenny. As he looked into her eyes, he forgot that she was a woman who carried a gun on her hip. He forgot that he'd once lost someone he loved because he, too, had worn a badge pinned to his chest.

"You're forgetting I'm an old, tough ex-Marine. Now if you'd stuck your tongue out at me, that would have been a different story. That would have really hurt my feelings."

Before Jenny realized it, she was laughing.

The sweet husky sound put a smile on Lucas's face, and he silently vowed he would do everything in his power to make Jenny laugh again and again. Until she finally realized it was okay to let herself be happy.

He drove several more miles west on the interstate. As Jenny watched the lights of the city fade behind them she asked, "Are we going to Tucumcari? Or are you going to stop somewhere in Texas?"

Chuckling, Lucas shook his head. "Be patient. I think you're going to like what I have to show you. And it isn't far now."

A few more miles passed before Lucas slowed the car and turned north onto a blacktopped road. As they drove through the rural area, Jenny noticed there was only a small scattering of house lights along the way. In several places she could barely discern herds of cattle bunched against the cedar breaks lining the road. In others, the land was open and tilled for planting.

"Have you ever been to this area?" Lucas asked.

"No. I rarely venture past the Oklahoma City limits."

Surprised, he glanced at her. "Well, surely you get out of the city sometimes. Don't you go on vacation? To visit friends or family?"

What family, Ruby? Sighing, Jenny twisted in the seat. "All my friends live here. And I don't have much family to speak of. But I do make two trips to Texas each year. I'm always glad to get back."

Lucas wondered if she was simply glad to get back to Oklahoma or glad to get away from whomever she visited.

"Do you go on vacations?" she asked him.

He shrugged. "Actually my job requires me to travel more than I like. But I enjoy going down to Florida to see my dad. You'd like that trip, too, I think. There's lots of birds and—''

"Snakes and alligators," she finished for him.

Surprised, he glanced at her. "You remembered."

"Yes," she answered.

The two of them lapsed into silence until Lucas turned off the road and headed down a long driveway. When he pulled the car to a stop in front of a huge old house, Jenny sat up in her seat and peered through the windshield.

"Is this where we're going? What is this place?"

"It's mine." He killed the motor and reached for Jenny's hand. "Come on. I want you to see the inside."

Next to the long porch, a massive sycamore and several elms stood like sentinels with bared arms. As the two of them walked up the wooden steps, Jenny imagined the place with the trees fully leafed and shading the old house. The porch would be cool and peaceful, a place to share a glass of lemonade or rock a baby.

"It'll be warmer inside," Lucas told her as he unlocked the door. "I keep it heated enough to prevent the pipes from freezing."

He stepped into the house and Jenny followed, careful to stay behind him until he'd flipped a switch and light flooded the room.

Jenny looked curiously around her. The room appeared to have once been a parlor. Several windows lined the east wall looking over the porch, while three more made up the south wall. In one corner was a stack of plasterboard. A small distance away stood two wooden sawhorses, a power saw and a large bucket filled with an assortment of carpentry tools.

"You can see I'm in the process of renovating this old thing." He took her by the elbow and guided her toward a doorway to their right.

"How long have you been working on it?" Jenny asked as he flipped another light switch.

"About three months. I know it would go faster if I hired more men on the job. But a buddy of mine who needs the extra cash has been helping me work on it at nights."

The two of them moved into a room that Jenny supposed would someday be the dining room. The wallpaper had been stripped and several boards were missing from the floor.

"You're doing part of the carpentry work?"

Laughing at the shocked note in her voice, he said, "I'm pretty good with my hands when I want to be. And working on this old house is a labor of love."

Yes, Jenny could see that as she watched Lucas rub his fingers along a new window facing. There was a look of pride and something akin to excitement on his face.

"I'm going to build a window seat along here. How do you think it would look?"

Jenny walked over to where he stood by the large bay window. "I'm afraid I've never lived in a house with a window seat." She laughed wryly. "Actually, I've never lived in a house before. So I'm not really the right person to ask."

Lucas felt an odd pain lance through his chest. How could it be that this woman had never lived in a house?

"Come here and look." With the sleeve of his jacket, he wiped a clean circle on the fogged windowpane. "It's pretty dark out tonight, but maybe you can see a little."

She walked to where he stood, then bringing her nose against the window, she cupped her hands around her eyes and peered into the darkness. "It looks like an old flower garden out there. I can see a birdbath and a rock border of some sort."

"I don't have much of a green thumb, but I think I can get something hearty going like marigolds and hollyhocks. Now can you imagine sitting on a window seat sipping your morning coffee and looking out at the birds and flowers?"

Jenny could imagine it all too well. It was just the sort of home she'd always wanted but knew she would never have.

"Sounds lovely," she murmured, then in an effort to shake her sudden melancholy, she turned and smiled at him. "But I didn't realize you were into things like birds and flowers."

Laughing, Lucas guided her away from the window. "Just because I once toted an M-16 and drove an eighteen-wheeler cross-country doesn't mean I don't know a meadowlark or a marigold when I see one. Even macho men like myself can enjoy nature."

"I see," she said, a smile in her voice. "Well, I must admit I know very little about birds or flowers."

They entered a short, wide hallway. Lucas took her hand and led her up a steep staircase.

As they climbed to the second floor, Lucas said, "I find that hard to believe, Jenny. You look like a woman who appreciates nature."

"I do. But you see, I grew up in southwest Texas. There wasn't much more than sagebrush and grama grass where I lived. Water was a scarce commodity, so we didn't use it to grow flowers or a Bermuda lawn. Besides, Ruby wouldn't have grown flowers or grass if she'd had buckets of water."

"Ruby?"

"My mother."

The flat tone of her voice told Lucas Ruby wasn't a topic Jenny wanted to discuss at the moment, so he decided not to ask her more. Instead, he hoped she would eventually *want* to talk to him about her personal life.

They reached the landing and Jenny could see where Lucas and his friend had been replacing floorboards.

"I plan to make all the bedrooms up here," he said, his face just inches behind her. "There're four of them so maybe that will be enough."

Enough? What was he doing, planning to turn the place into a country bed-and-breakfast?

"Lucas, do you plan to live here or what?" she asked, as they entered one of the bedrooms.

"Of course. What did you think I was going to do with it?"

Jenny shrugged as she looked around the room. Most of the work had already been completed. "I thought you might be going to make a country inn or a rental house."

"Oh, no. I searched long and hard for a place like this. I'm looking forward to living here."

She rubbed her hand against the cabbage rose wallpaper. "This is beautiful," she said, unaware of the wistful note in her voice.

Lucas moved across the room to stand a small step away from her. In spite of the cold night, she looked like a warm flame with her auburn hair and red coat. More than anything, Lucas wanted to pull her into his arms and feel the heat of her body, the scorch of her kiss.

The erotic thoughts put a husky rasp to his voice when he spoke. "I'm glad you like it. Women tend to place importance on the bedroom. I tried to keep that in mind when I chose the wallpaper."

Her brows arching with speculation, she lifted her eyes to his face. "Then you don't plan on living here alone?"

His dark eyes delving into hers, he said, "I hope not, Jenny. It's a big house for just one person. Someday I want to have a wife and children to fill these rooms."

Something inside Jenny's heart cracked and pain crept inside. She and Lucas were very nearly the same age. He was planning his future, dreaming of marrying and having children, while Jenny had put all that behind her. She was going to do five, perhaps ten more years of police work and then retire. After that, she planned to take enough schooling to become a counselor for battered women. She believed it was an admirable future and nothing to be ashamed of. But compared to Lucas's plans it seemed lacking.

While she was settling down to live the rest of her life alone, he was going to be having children, building a home. It didn't seem right. What had she done wrong to make her life be nearly over at the age of thirty-four? And why did it kill her to think of Lucas bringing some other woman to this beautiful house? Why did it claw at her insides to think of him having children with someone other than herself? Nothing made sense to her anymore.

"So you want a wife," she said finally.

"You sound surprised."

She let out a long breath. "You don't seem the marrying type."

One corner of his mouth lifted. "I don't?"

Up until now Jenny hadn't noticed how quiet and isolated they were. The only sounds to be heard were the wind outside, the creak of a giving board and their mingled breaths. Hers fast and shallow. His slow and deep.

Without warning, Jenny's heart began to pound. "If you were a marrying man, you would have found a wife a long time ago."

Lucas couldn't help himself. He reached out and touched a red curl lying against her shoulder. It was silky, and as beautiful as the curve of her lips, the deep green of her eyes. She made him drunk and she didn't even know it, he thought.

"I'm a choosy man, Jenny. When I say the words I do, it's going to be with the right woman. And it's going to be forever. So far I haven't found such a woman."

Jenny told herself to step away from him, to turn their conversation to something impersonal. But she couldn't make herself move. No more than she could make herself stop wanting to know more about him, to know what went on inside his head and his heart.

"Maybe you're expecting too much," she told him.

"At times I've wondered that myself," he said. "I know there's no such thing as a perfect woman. But I don't really want a perfect woman. I just want her to be perfect for me."

He moved a step closer, and Jenny involuntarily moved back until her shoulder blades were pressing against the rose-covered wall.

"And what kind of woman would that be?" Jenny asked huskily.

Leaning forward, he planted a hand on either side of her head. Jenny stood stock-still and tried not to panic at the strong, male arms circling her. He wasn't touching her. He wasn't hurting her. He was simply close to her, she reminded herself. She could deal with that.

"What kind of a woman?" he repeated. "Well, I'm looking for a strong woman. Someone who won't crumble if the going gets rough. I want her to be able to stand up and tell me to go to hell if I'm wrong, or kiss me and tell me I'm wonderful if I'm right. And I want her to love and need children the same way I do."

Jenny didn't say anything, and after a moment Lucas said, "You think I'm asking too much, don't you. But I have my reasons, Jenny. You see, I grew up without a mother. And I don't want that to happen to my children."

Suddenly what he was saying outweighed the fear of his nearness. Jenny's eyes swiftly came up to study his face. All along, she figured Lucas had been born into one of those perfect homes where mother and father and child lived in happy harmony. Obviously she'd figured wrong.

"You didn't have a mother?"

A grimace twisted Lucas's features. "I did for the first two years of my life. Then my parents got divorced."

Thrusting a hand through his hair, he moved away from her and walked to a window. Jenny quietly watched him, and for the first time she was thinking of him not as a rich businessman but simply as a man with needs and emotions.

"My mother was several years younger than my dad," he went on after a moment. "The age difference apparently created a lot of problems between them. In the end, he considered her too young and unstable to care for a child. So he fought for custody and won."

Pushing herself away from the wall, Jenny went to him. "If he gave you a stable home, you should be glad."

"I am glad. God knows where I'd be today if Dad hadn't insisted on raising me."

"So where is your mother now? Do you ever see her?"

His expression stoic, he shook his head. "She's dead, Jenny. She died shortly after I went to live with my dad."

Jenny was so surprised she gasped. "Oh, Lucas. What happened?"

"From what my dad and others have told me, she liked to party with her younger friends. After she lost me, everyone said she went even wilder. She blamed my dad for

losing her baby, and she tried to forget by drinking. One
night she and a few of her friends were partying at a nearby
lake. Drunk and nerveless, she climbed a bluff of rocks
and dove off. She never hit the water. Instead, she landed
on the rocks and died instantly of a broken neck."

Jenny shuddered at the horrible image. "How awful,
Lucas."

He shrugged. "I suppose it's like you told me about not
having a father. You can't miss what you never had."

Yes, it was true Jenny had always told herself she didn't
really miss having a father all these years. He'd been a
shiftless no-account. She was better off without him. Obviously Lucas had been telling himself the same thing
about his mother. But Jenny knew, as she figured Lucas
also knew, that what they'd both missed in their lives was
too immeasurable to be imagined.

"Do you blame her for dying and leaving you?" Jenny
asked.

Lucas shook his head. "No. I blame her for being too
weak, for not being brave enough to face life."

Not everyone could be brave about all things, she
wanted to tell him. Including her. She could face a robber
with a loaded handgun and keep her wits calm and col-
lected. But to think of marrying again made her pop out
in a cold, shaky sweat.

When she didn't say anything, Lucas took her by the
shoulder and urged her toward the door. "Let's take a
quick look at the rooms left up here and then we'll go
down to the kitchen."

A few minutes later, Jenny was surprised to see that the
renovation of the kitchen was nearly completed. Sparkling white cabinets with glass fronts lined one entire wall.
The floor had been tiled in black and white squares, and a

huge work island with a butcher-block top was situated a handy step away from the range.

Jenny sat on a stool by the work island while Lucas made coffee.

"I know I promised to get you home early," he said. "But there's still one more thing I'd like to show you before we leave. And since it's outside, I figured we could use a warm-up before braving the cold."

This morning Jenny would have laughed if anyone had told her she'd be having dinner with Lucas tonight. And even two hours ago, she would have insisted on going straight home from the restaurant and giving him a polite goodbye. But things had changed between this morning and now. She was beginning to get a glimpse of the man inside, and what she'd seen so far had drawn her to him.

"Lucas?"

He turned away from the coffee machine. "Yes?"

Jenny opened her mouth, then just as quickly shook her head. "Forget it," she said.

What in the world was she doing? Just because Lucas had talked to her about his family didn't mean she should open up about hers. But he knew what it was like to grow up in a less than perfect home. She had a feeling she could tell him about Ruby and he wouldn't look at her as if she was a piece of shunned garbage.

"Are you getting cold?" he asked quickly. "I'll turn up the heater."

He went to a portable heater and turned the switch to a higher level. When he returned to take a stool beside her, he asked, "How's that?"

"It's fine." She felt like a fool, and dropped her eyes from his face. After a moment she began to draw imaginary circles on the butcher block. "You know when you asked me earlier about visiting relatives?"

Lucas nodded.

She let out a heavy sigh. "Well, I should have told you then that I don't have any relatives to speak of."

Lucas's gaze traveled slowly over her face. There was a sad look of regret in her eyes, a hopeless droop to the corners of her lips. "You have your mother, don't you?"

A caustic laugh burst from Jenny before she could stop it. "Ruby? She might have given birth to me, but that's where her mothering stopped. A neighboring couple did more toward raising me than she ever did."

Lucas didn't know what to say. She hadn't had a father, and now he was hearing that her mother wasn't anything close to being a parent. "That must have been tough on you."

Shrugging, Jenny looked at his face. "Well, hanging around the Benitez house was far better than going down to the tavern with Ruby." Wrinkling her nose, Jenny shuddered. "I can still smell the stale beer and cigarette smoke and hear the crack of pool balls. When I was small she made me sit on the floor behind the bar and play with my dolls while she worked. Later, she put me to work washing glasses. Until I began to develop curves. Then she sent me home to stay by myself. Ruby never liked competition," she said, then closing her eyes, she rubbed her fingers across her forehead. "Damn it, I sound like a bitter, jealous daughter."

"No, you don't. Not to me," he said gently.

She kept her eyes closed, and Lucas went to the counter and poured two mugs full of coffee. When he placed hers on the work island next to her, Jenny looked up and thanked him.

"So you didn't move around while you were growing up?" Lucas asked as he settled himself on the stool beside her.

Jenny laughed wryly. "Are you kidding? Ruby's still working in the same little tavern. I guess she always will be." She took a careful sip of the hot coffee, then glanced at Lucas. "That's where she met my father, you know. At that dingy little dive outside of Fort Stockton. I don't know how he happened to be in the area. He wasn't a local. Ruby never got around to that part of the story. She always focused more on his running out on her."

"Have you ever seen or heard from him?"

Jenny shook her head. "No. I doubt he realizes I exist."

"Do you wish he did?"

"No."

Lucas didn't say anything to that. But he could only wonder if her father, or lack of one, was the reason she was so against men in general. Maybe she didn't want to marry because she was afraid her husband would take a walk like her father had all those years ago. Or maybe she'd already been married to a man who walked out on her?

What difference did it make? She was just a date, a beautiful distraction, he tried to tell himself. Tomorrow none of this would matter to him.

But for tonight, he had to know.

"Jenny, have you ever been married?"

Chapter Six

Like a sudden blast of icy wind, the question froze Jenny, and for a moment all she could manage to do was look at him while her insides shivered.

"Why?"

Lucas shrugged. "Just curious. You asked me, so I'm asking you."

Jenny had wanted to tell Lucas about Ruby and the kind of mother she'd been, but the last thing she wanted to do was to admit to him that she'd been married to an abusive man. He might understand about her mother, but he wouldn't understand about Marcus. He might even blame her for being a bad wife. And Jenny couldn't bear that. She'd lived through enough pain and humiliation, and did not want to endure more from this man.

Looking across the kitchen and away from Lucas, she said in a flat voice, "I—was married for five years."

Her admission shouldn't have surprised him. She was a beautiful, desirable woman. Men had probably pursued her since she'd been old enough to wear lipstick and bat her eyelashes. Still, a part of him was knocked sideways to know she'd once loved a man that much. And why had it ended after five years? She didn't seem like the sort of woman who, once she was married, would take the partnership lightly.

"What happened?"

Jenny winced inwardly at the question, but she did her best to keep her features unmoving, her voice even. "After we'd already married, Marcus and I learned we wanted different things from life. My career as a policewoman certainly didn't help our relationship, either."

"You weren't working as a cop when you first got married?" Lucas asked.

Jenny shook her head. "I was twenty-three and had just started training in the academy when I met Marcus. At that time he insisted he could deal with my being a police officer. He actually urged me to go after the career I wanted. A few months later, after we were married, all that changed. He couldn't handle the idea of his wife working so closely with other men."

Lucas snorted. "Looks to me like he would have been more concerned about you being shot or stabbed rather than worried that you might have an affair."

Jenny grimaced as unwanted memories filled her head. In the first part of their marriage, Marcus's unwarranted jealousy had been nothing more than verbal accusations and fits of sulking. But as the years passed things grew worse. Instead of flinging angry words at her, he began to throw and break things, then finally toward the end he tried to break her with threats backed up by the use of his fist.

Dear God, one man in her life had been almost more than she could mentally bear, she thought with an inward shudder. She certainly hadn't wanted two! And she'd never given Marcus reason to think she had. So why would she *ever* want a man in her life again?

Why, indeed, she asked herself as she looked at Lucas's black hair and warm brown eyes, the hard sensual curve of his lips and the broad width of his shoulders beneath his leather jacket.

She might want, she silently admitted to herself. But one thing was for certain, she'd never touch.

"Marcus had a big ego," she told Lucas after a moment, then turning a curious glance on him, she asked, "Is that what would have worried you about my job? The danger involved?"

Lucas nodded grimly. "I must tell you, Jenny, I lost a very good friend who was a policeman in Fort Worth where I grew up. Actually, he was more than a friend. He was like my brother. And losing him to a bullet is not something I'll likely ever forget."

The bitter loss on his face stirred something deep inside Jenny. Leaning closer, she placed her hand over his. "I'm sorry about your friend, Lucas. But dying is a risk every policeman takes when he's out on the streets. Believe me, it's something I live with every day. And it's one of the main reasons I avoid men. They can't deal with any part of a policewoman. I doubt you could, either."

Lucas was beginning to ask himself that very question. When he'd first met Jenny he had tried to think of her as simply a woman. Not an enforcer of the law. She'd been so beautiful and strong-minded that her mere presence had been overwhelming. So much so that he'd almost forgotten she was a cop. All he could think about was how much he wanted her in his life.

Well, he still wanted her, but now he was beginning to know her. Really know her. And he couldn't imagine what it would be like to watch her strap on a gun every day and walk out the front door. He'd never know if she'd be coming safely back to him. His friend Neil had been smart, a veteran cop, and still he'd been killed in the line of duty. How could he bear it if he fell in love with Jenny, then lost her so senselessly?

"Until I was faced with the problem, I don't really know how I would deal with having a woman cop for a wife." His eyelids lowered as he leaned toward her. "But I can tell you one thing."

"What?" she asked, her voice husky.

Reaching out, he cupped his hand against the side of her face. Jenny's breath caught in her throat, and she had to fight the urge to rub her cheek against his palm, to lean forward and place her lips on his.

"If you were my wife, I'd rather you died in bed of old age with me beside you than see you killed out on the streets."

His hand dropped from her face. Jenny looked away and swallowed at the sudden thickness in her throat. He was being honest with her. And Jenny had to respect him for that, at least. So why did she suddenly feel so overwhelmed with sadness?

Placing her coffee on the butcher block, she tossed her red hair over her shoulder, then moved her eyes to his face. "Thank you, Lucas," she said with soft finality.

"For what?"

She slid from the stool and jammed her hands in her coat pockets. "For the evening, the coffee and being honest with me. Now we know how it is with you and me."

His brows arched with surprise and he opened his mouth to speak. Jenny immediately cut him off.

"Not that there is a you and me," she added quickly. "Because there isn't. I'm just glad you understand we can never be more than friends."

"I do?"

Ignoring the innocent look of puzzlement on his face, Jenny walked to the electric heater and held her palms toward the glowing coils.

"Of course you do."

Like hell, Lucas thought. He already felt like more than a friend to Jenny. And he was beginning to get the impression that she was more than just a little attracted to him.

"Look, Jenny, not every man is like your ex-husband. Some of us do have the capacity to understand."

He left his seat and walked to her. Jenny tilted her head to look him in the face. The moment her eyes connected with his, her knees wavered.

"You just said you couldn't deal with having a policewoman for a wife."

"I was speaking theoretically."

"You were speaking your mind."

He let out an impatient breath. "If you remember correctly, I only asked you out to supper tonight. I didn't ask you to marry me."

Anger and embarrassment washed through Jenny and stained her face red. "I'm not delusional, Lucas."

He arched a brow at her. "No. You're not delusional. You're worried."

"I am?"

He was smiling at her, a smile that showed his teeth and dimpled his cheek. Jenny didn't know whether she wanted to smack him with a backhand or a kiss.

"Yeah," he answered. "I think you're worried because you like me. And you don't want to like any man."

He was so on the mark that Jenny was momentarily taken aback. Could he read her so clearly? Did he already know why she shunned any sort of intimacy with a man?

"I do like you, Lucas. At least, I did until now."

Laughing softly, he looped his arm through Jenny's and led her out of the warm kitchen. "Jenny, do you always take everything so literally?"

"No. And I don't normally go out with men. But you knew that," she said a little crossly.

Without warning, Lucas took her by the shoulders and swung her around to face him. Jenny gasped and pressed her hands defensively against his chest.

"I'm glad you came out with me tonight, Jenny," he said quietly, his face mere inches from hers.

His breath was a warm caress on her face, and beneath her palms, she could feel the strong rise and fall of his chest. For one reckless moment, Jenny longed to slide her hands up and link them at the back of his neck. She wanted to rise on tiptoe and taste his mouth, hold him close and trust him not to ever hurt her.

Lucas went on. "What I said back in the kitchen about marrying a policewoman? Well, I was speaking my mind for the present. But—"

Jenny shook her head while thinking how wrong Lucas had been a few minutes ago. She wasn't worried about liking this man. She was desperately afraid of loving him!

"I don't want to hear this, Lucas. It doesn't concern me."

Lucas groaned inwardly. Who was she trying to kid? Him or herself?

Tightening his grip on her shoulders, he said, "I admit that right now I think I'd have trouble dealing with the fear and the worry of my wife being a cop. But if I needed a certain woman in my life, if I loved her enough, I think I could learn to live with her job.''

Why was he telling her this? she wondered. Why was he trying to paint her a picture that could never be?

''Perhaps you'll be luckier than I was, Lucas, and you'll fall in love with a woman who has a safe, nine-to-five job behind a desk.''

Maybe Lucas could find that nice, safe partner someday, but he didn't think so. He was afraid this woman standing here in front of him had already latched onto his heart. Now he had to figure out what to do about it.

''You know, it's possible that your luck could change, too,'' he murmured.

With a soft, self-deprecating laugh, Jenny pulled away from his grasp. ''I've had my chance, and I can tell you I'd rather be a cop. It's a heck of a lot safer than being a wife.''

Lucas wanted to ask her what she meant by that, but it was getting late and he figured she'd already told him all she wanted him to know for now.

With a wan little smile, he reached up and adjusted her muffler more closely against her throat. ''Come on,'' he told her, ''I'll show you the last of this ponderosa and then I'll take you home.''

Moments later the two of them walked fifty yards or more away from the house to a long barn that had once sheltered animals and farming equipment.

Inside, Lucas pulled the strings on a few bare light bulbs hanging from the rafters. Standing in the middle of the dirt floor, Jenny looked curiously around her. Some carpentry work had also been started on this structure, but for the most part it was still just an old barn. She couldn't imagine what was so special about it.

''Are you going to start raising animals? Racehorses to run at Remington Park?'' she asked him.

Laughing, Lucas walked to where Jenny remained standing by a tumbledown hay manger. "Well, I do have enough pastureland out here to run a few head of thoroughbreds. But for right now this is where my other kids are going to stay for the summer."

Her brows drew together in a curious frown. "Your other kids? Have I missed something here? Do you have children from a past relationship?"

Still smiling, Lucas took her by the arm and led her toward the east end of the barn. "I may have sown a few wild oats when I was younger, Jenny," Lucas told her. "But not that wild. No, I'm talking about needy children without proper homes or parents to look after them. Once I take up residence in the farmhouse, I plan to board them here during the summer."

"Board them? What do you mean?" Jenny asked.

"I mean give them each a couple of weeks here at my summer camp."

A summer camp for children, she thought. Would he never stop surprising her? "I know there's lots of children who live in the city and never get to see the country, much less spend several days in it."

He nodded. "That's why I think this place would be such a big hit with the kids. I plan to have them fishing the ponds, riding horses, feeding the chickens and gathering eggs. All the things a country kid does."

"Wouldn't you have to have some sort of license to do that sort of thing?"

"You're right and I'll also need to hire trained supervisors to manage and care for the children. But I've already checked into all that and the state's social services are very receptive to the idea."

"I realize you're not a pauper, Lucas, but it will take an enormous amount of money to do what you're planning."

He nodded once again. "Yes, it will. But several companies I do business with have already pledged huge contributions throughout the coming years, so it's not like I'll be funding the whole thing out of my pocket."

The dirt they were walking on suddenly ended and they took a step onto a clean concrete slab. "So how many children do you plan to have here?" she asked.

"I think I can easily house ten, maybe fifteen in this building." He motioned toward the shadowy space in front of them. "In this area where the concrete flooring has already been run, I plan to have a kitchen, dining room and a regular family-type living room with a television, couches and fireplace. A lot of these kids don't know what it's like to live in a real home. And that's what I'd like to try to give them. Even if only for a few weeks at a time."

The man certainly had big dreams and an even bigger heart. Even for a man with money, it would be a big undertaking to care for children who weren't his own.

No matter what Jenny's fears told her to do, she couldn't look at Lucas and her ex-husband in the same light. Marcus had threatened to kill her if she ever got pregnant. Lucas was going out of his way to help a child, any child who needed him. The whole idea went straight to her heart.

"Why are you doing this, Lucas?" She glanced at him, her eyes softly searching his face. "I'm sure you could give your money to a children's charity and—"

"I could. But giving money just isn't enough for me, Jenny. I want to be around to see their faces. I want to know for myself whether they're happy or if they simply need someone to talk to. Just signing a check won't do that."

In other words, he wanted to be a surrogate father. Amazed by the whole idea, Jenny turned her gaze to the dusty rafters, then over the partially rotted timbers supporting the roof. The place was a far cry from being a summer camp for children. Even so, Jenny could easily imagine the sound of their squeals and laughter filling the room.

"Lilah mentioned something about you going to a shelter this morning. Is this what she was talking about?"

Lucas shook his head. "No. She meant a place in the city. For the past several months a crew of men have been renovating an old warehouse of mine. We expect it to be complete in a few weeks. I'm calling it the Ray Lowrimore House, after my father."

Jenny was overwhelmed. After the Halloween dance, she knew that Lucas gave to children's funds. But she would have never guessed his generosity or commitment to them went this far.

She shook her head, in awed disbelief. "You're a businessman, Lucas. I'm sure running L.L. Freight is time-consuming. Why would you want the added responsibility of caring for children who aren't even related to you?"

A brief smile touched his lips. "Believe me, I've been asked that before, Jenny. And I know a lot of people think I'm crazy for taking on such a task. But I've been blessed in my life. Even though I lost my mother and grew up not having much, I had a loving father to see that I was fed, sheltered, loved and guided down the right path."

"And you want to do for other children what your father did for you?"

Lucas nodded, then his smile turned a little sheepish. "I should confess, Jenny. I didn't always have such noble ideas. When I was much younger, I was just as self-centered as the next guy. I wasn't until I was in the marines and on duty in Guatemala that I fully appreciated what my father had done for me. There were so many hungry, orphaned children there, with no one, not even the government to care for them. I vowed to myself then that if I was ever in a position to help a child, I would."

"You've really surprised me, Lucas."

He cast her a wry grin. "I do have more than making money and womanizing on my mind. That is what you thought of me, isn't it? That day you wrote me the speeding ticket?"

Her face warm with color, she said, "Yes. I thought you were rich and arrogant and—" She stopped before the words "too damn sexy" could pass her lips.

His eyebrows peaked with curiosity. "And what are you thinking now, Jenny Prescott?"

Deciding to avoid his pointed question, Jenny smiled at him. "That you're obviously very proud of your father."

"If there's one person in this world I truly love, it's my father. Ray raised me without any help. Something I think is even harder for a man to do." A cocky grin suddenly twisting his lips, Lucas reached for her hand. "Now, what about the money-making, womanizing, speedster part of me?"

"The only thing I knew about you then was what I read on your driver's license," she said, wishing she didn't like the warmth of his fingers wrapped around hers, or the shaky sweetness that rushed through her every time he drew near.

"So what are you thinking now?" he persisted.

Jenny never knew her heart could be so out of control and she could still remain standing. "I'm thinking—that you've kept me out far later than you promised. And I'm going to be very cranky with Orville tomorrow."

"Poor Orville." His eyes softly worshiped her face.

"Poor me," she murmured.

Not making an effort to move away from her, he continued to drink in the sight of her full lips, the deep red glow of her hair and the desperate, almost hungry look in her eyes. He wanted to make love to her. Every fiber in his body was urging him to reach out and pull her into his arms.

But he couldn't make that move. She was a policewoman, not wife material. And she was far too precious to be just another affair. So what did that leave him with, other than a stomach full of frustrating knots?

"Well, the night has been worth it, hasn't it?" he asked.

"I'll have to see tomorrow, won't I?"

The coyness in her voice very nearly crumbled his willpower. For one reckless moment he considered pulling her into his arms and worrying about the right or wrong of it later. But the moment passed, and before he could change his mind, Lucas tugged on her elbow.

"Come on, Jenny," he said a little gruffly. "I think it's time we both got home."

"Jenny, the hamburger would do a lot more good in your stomach than on the plate."

At the sound of Orville's voice, Jenny pulled her gaze away from the plate-glass window to her partner sitting across from her. "Were you saying something, Orville?"

The young man banged his forehead with the heel of his palm. "Jenny, you haven't eaten three bites, and it's time for us to be getting back on the beat. What's the matter with you? Are you sick?"

She was sick, all right, Jenny thought miserably. Sick of
trying to put Lucas out of her mind and failing. Nearly a
week had passed since the night he'd taken her out to his
farmhouse. That night had been the last she'd seen or
heard from him, and she fiercely told herself she was glad.

Deep down, Lucas probably was a good man. But he
was still a man, just the same. And just because she happened to meet a man she liked it wasn't time for her to cast
away her lessons from the past and behave like a love-
struck fool. No, it was good for her that Lucas hadn't tried
to contact her. Even so, she couldn't help but feel like an
old, discarded rag.

"I'm not sick, Orville. Just not hungry." Quickly she
tossed her dirty napkin and empty foam cup onto her
plate. "Come on. Let's get out of here."

The two of them dumped their trays and left the fast-
food restaurant. In the patrol car Orville reached to start
the motor, then paused to cast a concerned look at Jenny.

"You know," he said thoughtfully, "you've been looking sorta peaked the past couple of days. Have you been
sleeping all right?"

"Darn it, Orville! If you'd watch the streets as closely
as you do me, you might see something of importance!"
she snapped at him.

Unmoved by her remark, Orville started the engine and
merged onto the busy noonday street. "You are important, Jenny. You're my partner. If you're only giving fifty
percent of yourself instead of a hundred, I'm the one lia-
ble to suffer for it. I mean, it's not likely we're going to get
into a high-speed chase with a couple of bank robbers in
the next couple of minutes. But if we did—well, I'd feel a
lot safer about things if you weren't sitting over there with
a moony look on your face."

A moony look? Jenny wanted to shout he was a bumbling idiot. But she didn't. Instead she started counting to ten. By the time she reached nine, she felt like a heel.

"You're right, Orville. And I'm sorry if I haven't seemed with it these past few days. Something has—well, I've had a lot on my mind. But there's no need for you to be worried. If we get into a spot, I won't let you down. I promise you that."

They traveled a few blocks before Orville spoke again.

"You know, it's not just myself I'm worried about. I don't want anything to happen to you, Jenny."

She stared out the car window, her jaw set with firm resolution. "Don't worry, Orville. I'm not going to let anything happen."

Later that night when Jenny got off duty, she changed out of her uniform at the precinct station, then drove across town to Savanna's. It had been a long week, and she couldn't stand the thought of facing another evening in her empty apartment.

Savanna's husband, Joe, answered the door and ushered Jenny into the house.

"Savanna is in the kitchen making sauerkraut and wieners," he told her.

Jenny glanced at her wristwatch. "At this hour?"

Joe laughed. "She had a sudden craving."

Jenny rolled her eyes heavenward. "I hope for your sake she doesn't get these cravings in the wee hours of the morning."

"Oh, it's pretzels then," he said with humor. "But I'm getting used to waking up to the sound of munching and crumbs jabbing me in the back."

Jenny patted his shoulder. "I'll remind her what a good husband she has."

"Thanks," he said with a grateful smile, then motioned toward the kitchen. "Go on back there. She'll be excited to see you."

Jenny found Savanna sitting at the breakfast bar eating kraut and wieners. A name-your-baby book was propped open in front of her plate.

"Jenny!" she exclaimed with pleasure when she spotted her friend entering the room. "Come over here and have some sauerkraut with me. It's delicious. And not a bit fattening, thank goodness."

Jenny climbed up on the stool beside the blonde. "What's this I hear about you torturing Joe with pretzels in bed?"

Savanna giggled. "I don't torture him. I don't even turn on the lamp."

"You just chomp them in the dark and let the crumbs fall where they may," Jenny said with a teasing grin.

"I'm not that bad," Savanna insisted with a laugh, then shoveled up a forkful of kraut and popped it into her mouth. "I never knew how much I loved this stuff until I got pregnant."

"How have you been feeling? Other than hungry?"

"Fine. Wonderful." Savanna glanced at her between bites. "How are you? You looked peaked."

Jenny frowned. "You sound like Orville."

"So he noticed, too?" Savanna lay her palm against Jenny's forehead. "Has the flu bug been going around down at the station?"

"Oh, stop it! I'm not peaked or ill," Jenny said with annoyance. "I just haven't been sleeping well lately. I've had a lot on my mind."

Her plate empty, Savanna carried it to the sink and rinsed it beneath a stream of water. "Couldn't be that trucking tycoon you were telling me about is keeping you up at night?''

With a weary groan Jenny slid off the stool and joined Savanna at the sink. "I haven't even seen the man. Not since—we went out to dinner the other night."

Savanna was suddenly bubbling with excitement. "You went out to dinner with the man? Jenny, that's wonderful! Where did he take you? What happened? Tell me all about it!"

Jenny's first instinct was tell Savanna that nothing had happened that night. But she realized that wouldn't quite be telling the truth. Something had happened. Lucas had shown her a glimpse of his future, and in doing so, Jenny had caught a glimpse of her own. And the sight had left her lonely and afraid.

Propping herself against the counter, Jenny quickly described the dinner she and Lucas had shared, then went on to tell about the trip to the old farmhouse and all the things she'd learned about him there.

"So the man wants to marry and have children," Savanna mused. "That's encouraging."

Jenny shook her head. "Don't let those wheels of yours start racing," she told Savanna. "I'm not ever going to marry again. And even if I did consider it, Lucas has a thing about cops. A close friend of his was killed in the line of duty. He doesn't believe he could deal with a wife being on the police force."

Savanna's eyes grew wide and calculating. "You talked about that?"

"Only in theory," Jenny assured her, then groaned with frustration. "Oh, I don't know why I'm telling you any of this. There's nothing really between us. I don't even *want* anything to be between us."

"Bull!"

A kettle on the stove suddenly let out a whistle. Savanna filled a ceramic teapot with boiling water, then dropped in several bags of decaffeinated tea.

"There's no bull about it," Jenny replied. "I'm using good old common horse sense here. And it tells me that I'd be a fool to let my heart get mixed up with the man. Besides, I haven't even heard from him. That tells you how interested he is in me."

"And you're obviously disappointed."

Jenny opened her mouth to protest, but nothing came out. For the past few days she'd been lying to herself, telling herself she wasn't really waiting for his call or to hear his knock on her apartment door. Maybe it was time she quit lying to herself and to Savanna.

"Okay, so I have missed him," she said glumly, then groaning helplessly, she closed her eyes and rubbed them with the tips of her fingers. "I don't understand why he made such a big issue of wanting to know me and then— Oh, I wish there wasn't even such a thing as the male species. It would make life much simpler."

"Speak for yourself," Savanna said cheerfully.

Jenny frowned at her. "Well, that's easy for you to say. You have a wonderful husband who loves you."

Savanna placed the teapot, two cups and milk and sugar on a tray, then carried it to where Jenny sat holding her forehead.

"Jenny, Jenny," Savanna scolded. "I'm worried about your memory. You seem to forget that less than a year ago I was crying my eyes out over Joe. At that time in my life I believed I didn't want to marry him or any man."

"You came to your senses."

"Only because you helped me open my eyes and see what I really wanted in life."

"I already have everything I want," Jenny countered.

"Then what are you squawking about?"

Jenny remained silent as she watched Savanna pour the tea. What was she squawking about? she asked herself.

"I don't know, honey. I—" She shook her head with helpless resignation. "Savanna, when Lucas was showing me that old house and talking about filling it with his children, I—I'd never felt more sad or alone. I thought about you and Joe and Megan and the new baby on the way and I kept wondering why I had to ruin my life over someone like Marcus. Why couldn't I have met Lucas back then? Back before Marcus turned me into something less than a woman?"

"If you're expecting sympathy from me, Jenny, you're not going to get it. Marcus didn't turn you into something less than a woman. You only think he did. You're beautiful and sexy and intelligent. And it's never too late to start over. To try again."

Jenny's eyes clouded with despair. "I'm thirty-four years old, Savanna. I'd be crazy to take a risky chance with what future I have left."

Ignoring her tea for the moment, Savanna reached over to cover Jenny's hand with her own. "What sort of future will you have if you don't?"

Jenny dumped two spoons of sugar into her teacup, then gave it a vicious stir. "I'll tell you what kind of future I'll have," she answered. "I'll have a safe, predictable future. And that's what I want the most."

Savanna rolled her eyes with frustration. "Then, my dear, you'd better forget all about Lucas Lowrimore."

With a grim set to her jaw, Jenny lifted the teacup to her lips. "That's exactly what I intend to do," she said.

And she would, Jenny assured herself. As soon as she figured out how to do it.

Chapter Seven

The next evening Jenny and Orville were cruising May Avenue when the dispatcher came over the radio with a domestic disturbance. Being the nearest officers in the vicinity, the two of them answered the call.

In the few minutes it took to reach the scene, Jenny drew in several calming breaths and tried to steel herself for what was ahead.

"You hate these things, don't you?" Orville asked as he wheeled the patrol car through a busy intersection.

She darted a glance at her partner. "Don't you?"

He nodded grimly. "I guess every officer does."

"Well, at least the man isn't armed with a gun." It was the only positive thing Jenny could say.

"Sometimes fists are just as bad."

"Yes, I know," she said. And it was something she'd spent the past five years trying to forget.

The domestic call turned out to be an ugly scene. Several minutes passed, though to Jenny it seemed like hours, before they finally managed to handcuff the combatant husband and calm the bruised, weeping wife. By the time Jenny wrote out the arrest report later that evening, then drove home, she was as limp as a dirty dishrag.

What's the matter with me? Jenny asked herself as she stepped tiredly into her apartment. In the past ten years, she'd been on many domestic calls. Some of them far rougher than this one tonight. It was a part of her job, and she'd learned to deal with the ugliness of it. So why had the sight of that battered woman shaken her to the very core of her being? Why was she still sick inside? And most of all, why did she feel so damn useless?

In the bedroom, she unbuckled her weapon and tossed it onto the foot of the bed. Then, unbuttoning her shirt, she walked over to the dresser mirror and studied the tired image staring back at her.

She was a police officer, she thought angrily. She should be able to do more to help women like that—like she'd once been. It was one of the reasons she'd gone into the police academy in the first place. Because she thought she could make a difference. What a joke!

Leaning closer to the mirror, she rubbed her fingertips over the dark hollows beneath her eyes. She wasn't the same Jenny Prescott she'd been three weeks ago. At that time, she'd been satisfied with her job. Now she was beginning to wonder if she'd been a fool all these years to think she could help even one battered woman. Worse than that, she was beginning to wonder if she'd simply been hiding behind a badge and a gun for ten years.

Damn his hide, it was all Lucas's fault, she muttered to herself as she stepped into the shower. If he hadn't come along and messed with her mind, she'd still be a contented woman. Lonely, maybe, but that was an easy price to pay compared to the turmoil she was going through right now.

More than an hour later Jenny was lying on the couch, trying to get interested in a movie, when a knock sounded at the door.

Frowning, Jenny glanced at the digital clock on the VCR. It was too late for any of her friends to be calling, and if Captain Morgan needed her, he'd simply telephone.

Tossing her tumbled hair out of her face, Jenny walked barefooted to the door.

"Who is it?" she asked cautiously.

"Lucas."

Lucas! Her hand fluttered to her throat. What was he doing here? Tonight, at this ridiculous hour? And why was her heart suddenly pounding with pleasure? She was sure she'd convinced herself she never wanted to see him again.

"Are you going to let me stand out here till the sun rises?"

Flustered, Jenny fumbled with the bolt lock. When she finally managed to get the door open Lucas was standing on the other side, his black hair rumpled by the wind, his cheeks dimpled with a sheepish little grin.

"I know it's late," he said, stepping into the apartment.

Jenny shut the door behind him, then turned. "Late! Lucas, it's the middle of the night!"

He shrugged. "I'm sorry. But I couldn't wait to see you."

Her eyes wide with disbelief, she echoed, "Couldn't wait? It's taken you over a week to decide if you wanted to see me again? And then it suddenly hit you around midnight to come over here?"

Lucas's dark eyes slid over her outraged face, her tumbled mass of red hair, then more slowly over her silk pajamas and the sensual curves beneath them. She was the most desirable, beautiful woman he'd ever known, and for the past week her memory had consumed him. Cop or not, he had to have her in his life. It was that simple.

"I'm afraid you've got it wrong. It's taken me a week to get back to town. I had to go to Chicago for a few days, then on to Cleveland."

"I take it there wasn't any telephones in either city?"

Laughing, Lucas reached for her hand. In spite of herself, Jenny gave it to him, then felt her heart immediately turn over as he pressed his lips against her palm.

"So you wanted me to call," he said with lazy pleasure. "That's encouraging, Jenny. Real encouraging."

Pulling her hand from his grasp, she marched over to the couch, picked up the remote and smashed the off button. "You know what I meant, Lucas. You go for a week without even bothering to call, then you show up in the middle of the night like—an eager lover. You must think I was born yesterday!"

Lucas shrugged out of his leather jacket, walked over to the couch and tossed it over the back.

"I didn't call because I wanted to give us both time to ponder about things. And no, I don't think you were born yesterday. I believe you're glad to see me," he said with irksome confidence. "Even though you don't want to admit it."

"I'm not glad to see you," she said, her heart fluttering as he came to stand in front of her.

"You're lying," he said, his hands curving over the top of her shoulders. "I think you've missed me this week. The same way I've missed you."

His fingers burned through the silk pajama top. Jenny could only wonder if they would feel that hot against her bare skin. "Lucas, I—"

His eyes glinting, he lowered his head toward her. "I can see you're a woman who has to be shown instead of told. And I think it's high time I did some showing."

In the back of her mind, Jenny knew what was coming, but she couldn't seem to lift a finger to stop it. Then it was too late. His lips were on hers, and she was irretrievably lost.

Other than a friendly peck on the cheek, it had been years since Jenny had been kissed by a man. And even then it hadn't been like this. Her head was spinning, her heart pounding madly as his lips tasted hers, his hands crushed her hips against his.

With a groan of surrender, Jenny curled her arms around his neck and welcomed the intimate invasion of his tongue between her teeth.

Long moments passed before Lucas finally pulled his mouth away from hers. When he did, Jenny's head lolled weakly against the crook of his arm.

"Dear Lord, it's a good thing I hadn't done that before I left, or I could have never stayed away from you a whole week," he said, his voice husky with desire.

Her breathing still ragged, she opened her eyes to see his face was still only inches from hers. Trying to rally her senses, she levered a wider distance between them.

"Why did you do that?"

"Because I've wanted to do it for weeks. And because you needed it."

Jenny's mouth fell open. "I needed it? That northern air you've been breathing this past week must have done something to your brain."

His hands hugged her waist. "The air didn't, but the time away from you did. It cleared up my thinking."

Her expression was skeptical. "You've had trouble with your thinking?"

Lucas nodded solemnly. "Ever since you walked up to my car with that clipboard in your hand, I've had serious problems."

So had she, Jenny thought miserably, and it looked like they were growing worse by the minute. "How so?"

"I took one look at you and knew I'd found that strong, beautiful woman I'd been searching for. I just hadn't planned on you being a cop."

Her tongue darted out to moisten her lips. "Well, I am a cop. And as far as I'm concerned we were nothing more than friends when we parted the other night. I can't see that anything has changed since then."

One corner of his mouth cocked upward. "We were more than friends the day you wrote me the traffic ticket."

Her nostrils flared as his fingers slid slowly up her back. "You're right, we were enemies."

He chuckled softly, then suddenly his face went quietly serious as he leaned closer and pressed his cheek against hers.

"You know that I love you, Jenny."

A strange mix of joy and fear dashed through Jenny like a stormy surf. Lucas loved her! It was wonderful and it was absolutely terrifying.

As her silence grew, Lucas pulled his head back to look at her. "Don't you have anything to say?"

Hoping it would ease the pounding of her heart, Jenny drew in a deep breath. It didn't help. "Lucas, you can't love me! You—don't even know me. You've just now kissed me!"

A grin spread across his face. "Well, it wasn't for lack of wanting to, I can tell you that! But if more kissing will prove it, I'll be glad to oblige."

"Lucas—"

Before Jenny could say more, he was kissing her again. The slow, seductive search he made of her lips was completely mesmerizing. Heat pooled deep within her, and before Jenny realized it, her hands gripped his shoulders, urged him closer.

"You know, you're right," he eventually whispered against her lips. "Kissing does tell the tale. And it's telling me I want to be kissing you even when this beautiful red hair of yours has turned silver, your face is wrinkled, and you have a little potbelly."

He patted her tummy for emphasis, and tears began to well in Jenny's eyes. With an anguished groan, she twisted out of his embrace and stood with her back to him.

"Maybe you feel like that now—" She looked down and covered her face with both hands.

Lucas could hear pain in her voice, but he didn't know why it was there. He'd just told the woman he loved her, and he believed she felt the same way about him. So why was she acting like he'd just given her a death sentence?

Stepping closer, he cupped his hands around her shoulders. "Jenny, I know this probably seems sudden to you, but—"

"No! It seems impossible to me!"

His eyes lifted helplessly to the ceiling. "Are you trying to say you don't love me? It didn't feel that way a few moments ago when we were kissing."

Shards of pain sliced through every part of Jenny. "I tried to tell you, Lucas—I tried to discourage you. I told you I didn't want a man in my life. Now here you go telling me you love me and—"

He gently turned her to face him. "And you might as well get used to it. Because I'm not going to go away."

Groaning, Jenny shook her head. "I'm a cop, Lucas. You've already told me you couldn't deal with that."

"This past week without you has shown me I can deal with anything to keep you in my life. You were a cop when I fell in love with you, and if you remain on the force, I'll still love you just as much. You've got to believe I won't be like your ex—''

At the mention of Marcus, Jenny's eyes turned to twin pieces of granite. "You don't know about him! You don't know about me! If you did, you wouldn't be saying any of this."

Impatient, Lucas gave her shoulders a little shake. "What do you mean, Jenny? Were you and he partners in some sort of crime? Do you honestly think you could tell me anything that would change my feelings for you?"

Jenny suddenly felt as if her knees were going to buckle beneath her. Leaning heavily against Lucas, she whispered weakly, "I've got to sit down."

Quickly, Lucas helped her to the couch, then took a seat on the cushion next to her.

"Do you want a drink of water?" He worriedly scanned her pale face. "Something else?"

Jenny shook her head, then swallowed. "No. I just—" She forced her eyes to meet his. "I never committed any sort of crime, Lucas. But there was a time in my life that I wanted to. There was a time I wanted to kill my husband!"

Lucas could see that she wasn't just mouthing words, that she truly meant them, and suddenly everything fell into place. "He hurt you."

Shame caused Jenny to look down. "Yes," she said quietly. "Many times."

Just hearing her admit what happened made Lucas want to track the man down and strangle him with his bare hands.

"Why did you stay with him for five years? That's a long time."

Jenny had been asked that very question time and again. The same way she figured other battered women had been asked.

"At first I loved Marcus. And he loved me, or at least he appeared to love me. But after about a year of marriage, Marcus's job of selling real estate began to suffer. By the time it hit rock bottom, he was taking his frustration out on me. He turned dominating and wanted to control every move I made. At the time, I truly believed his attitude stemmed from his job, and because I loved him, I tried to give him the support and understanding I thought he needed. But the more I tried to help him, the more belligerent and controlling he became with me."

"Then he wasn't actually hitting you during those five years of marriage?" Lucas asked, his expression grim.

With a heavy, woeful sigh, she shook her head. "No. It wasn't until the last year of our marriage that he became physically violent. By then, I'd been a police officer for nearly four years. I'd arrested men just like Marcus. But still I couldn't bring myself to raise a hand to him or report him to the police. Dear God, I *was* the police! Yet I wasn't able to handle my own husband! It was so humiliating. You'll never know how helpless and ashamed I felt, Lucas. Never!"

She was right, of course. Lucas wouldn't ever know how she'd felt then, but he could imagine the fear and isolation she must have endured. And it broke his heart.

"What made you finally divorce him?" he asked quietly.

Jenny's gaze dropped to the floor. "I guess it was a combination of things. I finally began to see that no matter how perfect I tried to be, Marcus wasn't going to be satisfied. So I gave him an ultimatum. He'd either get help or I was going to divorce him. His response was to whack me around the room and tell me he didn't have a problem, I was the one with the problem. And he said if I tried to divorce him, he'd kill me."

"But you ended the marriage anyway." Lucas stated the obvious.

Looking at him, Jenny nodded. "I was a police officer. I'd seen men like Marcus before and knew what they were capable of doing to a woman. I knew if I didn't get out of the situation, he could very well wind up killing me. He'd certainly already killed my love for him."

Lucas reached for her hand and found it to be ice cold. "That must have taken a lot of courage."

"I don't know about that, Lucas. I think after a while a woman goes through so much pain she finally becomes anesthetized. I didn't care if he tried to kill me. I wanted out at any cost."

He squeezed her hand. "Well, surely you can't feel guilty because you once harbored thoughts of doing him harm? It's only human nature to want to fight back and defend yourself. Besides, you never actually hurt him, did you?"

Bitterness twisted her face. "No. I turned him loose on some other poor, unsuspecting woman."

"Where is Marcus now?" he asked gently.

"God only knows. I wouldn't be surprised to hear he's in prison somewhere."

Lucas let out a long breath, then said, "Oh, Jenny, I'm so sorry this ever happened to you."

"I don't want you to be sorry, Lucas. I just want you to understand why I've chosen never to marry again."

Lucas reached for her other hand and clasped them both tightly between his. "I can understand why you might be afraid to try marriage again. But surely you can see that I would never be like Marcus.''

No, she didn't think Lucas would ever raise his hand against a woman. But there were other ways to hurt people without banging them around the room. And she'd already endured enough pain to last her a lifetime.

''Marcus was a nice guy when I was dating him,'' she told Lucas. ''And even while we were married, he was the good old boy on the block. He was charming to all our neighbors and friends. He would go out of his way to help any of them. No one would have ever suspected the wrath he unleashed on me. I guess that's why I blamed myself for so long. Since it was only me that angered him, it must have been my fault.''

It hurt Lucas to think she had ever blamed herself. It hurt him even more to imagine she could compare him to the sick man who'd once been her husband. He loved her so much. All he wanted to do was make her happy.

''And you believe I could be the same way?''

''No. Not really. But I—'' Drawing her hands from his, she rose from the couch and walked quickly to the kitchen area.

Lucas followed and found her leaning over the sink, her head in her hands. ''Jenny?''

At the sound of his voice, she turned to face him. Lucas could see traces of tears on her cheeks.

''Lucas, you don't understand,'' she said. ''It's not that I look at you and think if I marry you, you'll start hitting me. I don't think you would.''

Relieved, Lucas closed the small space between them and framed her face with both hands. ''Then what's wrong? Why are you trying to shut me out before I have a chance to show you how much I love you?''

Jenny tried to swallow the painful lump in her throat. "You don't understand what living with Marcus did to me. My heart doesn't work right anymore, Lucas. It's hard and cold and suspicious. You see, it had to become that way to survive. And I don't think it can change. Not for you or any man."

"You're wrong, Jenny. Your heart isn't hard and cold. You love me. And I'm going to prove it to you."

Bending his head, he kissed away the salty tears on her lips. "Good night," he murmured, then brushed his knuckles against the soft point of her chin.

Lucas was a good man, she thought, as he walked to the couch and shrugged into his leather jacket. But he wasn't that *one* good man who could turn her life into happily ever after. There wasn't such a man for Jenny.

Her eyes blurred with tears, she watched him quietly leave the apartment.

The next evening when she and Orville returned from their patrol duty, she found a note on her desk. It was from Lucas's secretary, Lilah. The woman wanted Jenny to call her as soon as it was convenient.

Ignoring the telephone number on the bottom of the square of paper, Jenny tapped her fingers against the metal desk. Why would Lilah be contacting her, she wondered. Had Lucas put her up to something?

It didn't matter if he had, Jenny decided after a moment. She was going to call Lilah and make sure he got the message once and for all that she was off-limits where he was concerned. Maybe he did think he loved her now, but he'd get over it. He was young and rich and good-looking. It wouldn't be a problem at all for him to find another woman.

Trying not to dwell on the "other woman" part, Jenny punched in the telephone number and waited for an answer.

"Lilah's residence."

Jenny was immediately taken aback. She hadn't expected this to be Lilah's personal number.

"Lilah? This is Jenny Prescott. I'm sorry I'm bothering you at home. I thought this was your work number."

"Honey, don't apologize. I'm the one who should be apologizing for calling you at work, but I didn't know any other way to reach you."

"That's quite all right. Was there something I could do for you?"

"Just a minute, love, I've got B.B. King on the stereo and Lucille is getting a little carried away."

Jenny could hear her put down the phone, then the blues music in the background was muted to a softer level.

"There. Now I can hear you," Lilah said when she returned. "Actually, there is something you can do for me. What are your plans for Thanksgiving?"

Thanksgiving? Jenny hadn't even realized that time of year was near. All she knew was that it was cold and dreary and spring was a long time away.

"I don't have any plans, Lilah. I'm not even sure if I'm listed on the work roster that day. More than likely, I am."

"That's just not good at all," she replied. "You've got to find out and let me know as quickly as possible. I want you to have Thanksgiving dinner with me."

Jenny couldn't believe her ears, then suddenly she could. "Is Lucas going to be there?"

Lilah laughed as though her question was ridiculous. "Of course, honey. Lucas's daddy is way off in Florida and he doesn't have a mother. Well, I mean other than me. So naturally he always has Thanksgiving dinner at my house. And I remember you saying you didn't have any family in the area, so I thought it would be nice for you to join us."

Jenny hated to sound rude, but she had to ask. "Did Lucas put you up to this?"

Lilah laughed again. "I haven't even seen Lucas today, and as busy as he stays, I'll have to remind him that Thursday is Thanksgiving."

There was only one answer Jenny should give the woman. She should simply thank her for the invitation and decline. But she couldn't make herself utter the words. Other than Savanna, who was going out of town for Thanksgiving, no one had thought of her or cared that she might be spending the holiday alone. To think that Lilah did touched Jenny.

"Give me a moment, Lilah, and I'll go check the duty roster."

"Take your time, honey. I'll hold."

Jenny walked to the bulletin board at the back of the room. As soon as she found Thursday's schedule, she hurried back to the telephone.

"Lilah, I'm afraid I don't get off work until one that afternoon. But it was nice of you to think of me anyway."

"Can you make it by two?"

Jenny was so surprised by the question, she glanced at the receiver in her hand. "Yes, I could. But, Lilah, I wouldn't hear of putting you out that way. There's no point in delaying your dinner just so I can be there."

"Nonsense. With dinner being at a later hour, I won't have to get up before dawn to put the turkey in the oven. I'll be able to have coffee in bed and do it later. It'll be lovely."

Jenny knew it was utter foolishness to go to a dinner when she knew Lucas would be there. But she could count on one hand the times she'd had a traditional Thanksgiving dinner. She wasn't going to let Lucas put her off this one.

"Thank you for inviting me, Lilah. I'll be there. Do I need to bring anything?"

"Just your smiling face. So here's my address." She gave Jenny directions to her house, then added, "See you Thursday."

Jenny thanked her again, then thoughtfully hung up the telephone.

Was she out of her mind? she wondered. Or was she really a masochist? Had she stayed with Marcus all those years because she liked being dominated and abused? Was that why she was setting herself up for more suffering?

Angry at the questions she was posing, Jenny snatched up a report form and scrolled it into the typewriter. Damn it, she was going to get to work and quit analyzing herself. It didn't matter why she was going to have Thanksgiving dinner at Lilah's. She was simply going to go and enjoy it.

Two days later, Jenny drove to the address Lilah had given her. The area was a quiet neighborhood of houses that had been built in the happy, prosperous fifties.

A black pickup was parked in the short driveway. Jenny parked behind it, then walked to the small porch snuggled between two tall evergreens. Brown-gold leaves from a nearby sycamore tumbled across the yard, then sailed toward her feet.

Just as she reached for the doorbell, a gust of wind caught the tail of her crinkled gauze skirt and sent it flying above her waist.

"Good afternoon, Jenny. Need a little help with that?"

Gasping at the sound of Lucas's voice, she grabbed the flying material and shoved it in place. But from the grin on his face, Jenny knew he'd already caught an eyeful of thighs and calves.

Her cheeks pink, she brushed past him and stepped into the house. "A gentleman would have turned his head," she said primly.

He shut the door behind him, then took her shoulder and spun her into his arms. "It just isn't in me to be a gentleman, Jenny."

Before she could manage to draw a breath, his lips were on her mouth, his hands on her hips, tasting, tempting, turning her insides to liquid heat.

After what seemed an eternity, he finally moved her away from him, and Jenny stared at him, her chest heaving. "Do you think I came here for that?" she gasped between panting breaths.

Lucas smiled at her stunned look. "I'm sure you're going to tell me you're here for the turkey and giblet gravy."

"And Lilah's company," she added in her no-nonsense cop voice.

He began to laugh. Jenny glared at him.

"What are you doing now? Trying to insult your secretary?" she asked.

"Insult Lilah?" He laughed again. "Why, when I found out she'd invited you to have dinner with us today, I kissed her four times. She loved it."

Even though her insides were still glowing from his kiss, Jenny rolled her eyes at him. "I'm sure."

A smug little smile on his face, Lucas took her by the elbow and led her out of the short foyer. "Lilah appreciates a man's attention," he said. "She's gone through more beaus in the past five years than I have shirts."

"Where is Lilah, anyway?" Jenny asked, as they stepped down into a long sunken living room. "Have you tied and gagged her and thrown her into a closet?"

As they walked across the room to a group of furniture, he hummed a bar of Elvis's song about suspicion. "You do have a cop's mind, don't you?"

She looked at him as they took a seat on the chintz-covered couch. "I've learned you're a man who'll do a lot of maneuvering to get what he wants."

He laughed. "Well, as much as I'd like to be alone with you, I haven't gagged Lilah and tossed her into the closet. She's in the kitchen getting the last of the meal ready."

"Shouldn't we be helping her?"

Lucas shook his head. "You stay out of Lilah's kitchen just like you stay out of her files. She has her own way of doing things."

The sound of a door opening caught Jenny's attention. She turned to see Lilah entering the room carrying a tray of hors d'oeuvres.

"There you are, Jenny, dear. I thought I heard voices." She placed the tray on the coffee table in front of Jenny and Lucas. "I thought you two might like to nibble while I finish putting everything on the table."

"I'll be glad to help," Jenny offered. She started to rise from the couch. Lilah quickly motioned her down.

"You just keep Lucas out of my hair. That will be help enough."

"Lilah, what are you talking about? I couldn't get in that beehive with a jackhammer," he told the older woman.

Not a bit insulted, she patted his cheek. "No, but you can get into my cooking pots."

She swished her way out of the room. Lucas leaned forward and took a cracker from the tray. While he dipped it into something creamy, Jenny said, "You two have a strange relationship for a boss and secretary. I noticed that at work she calls you Mr. Lowrimore and here she calls you Lucas."

Lucas shrugged. "She likes us to be professional at work. And away from it, I let her be my mother and she lets me be her son."

Jenny looked at her clasped hands and thought of all the times she wished she'd had someone like Lilah. Someone to give her the courage to free herself of Marcus's abuse. "That must be nice. To be that close to someone."

"It is."

The lost, yearning look on her face reminded Lucas of the children he met with in the park. "I'm sure you have many friends, too, Jenny."

She glanced at him. "I have several friends in the department. My closest friend, Savanna, went to New Orleans to spend Thanksgiving with relatives. But I don't have anyone like Lilah."

"Your mother doesn't invite you to spend the holidays with her?"

Jenny let out a harsh laugh. "I doubt Ruby knows how to turn on the oven. Much less bake a turkey."

He took a bite of the cracker. "I've noticed you call her Ruby instead of Mother."

Jenny shrugged. "That's the way she wants it. It makes her feel too old, you see, to have a thirty-something-year-old daughter call her Mother."

Lucas shook his head. "Sounds like a hell of a woman. Why do you even acknowledge her?"

Her eyes remaining on her lap, Jenny said, "I admit Ruby isn't much of a mother. But she could have chosen not to give birth to me, even all those years ago. And she always kept a roof over my head and food in my mouth. That's more than a lot of kids get. You should know that, Lucas."

Yes, Lucas did know it. But just like the kids he tried to help, Jenny had deserved more than food and shelter while she'd been growing up. She deserved more than that now. And he desperately wanted to be the one to give it to her.

He dipped another cracker and offered it to Jenny. She shook her head, so he ate it himself.

"I want you to know," he told her, "I didn't have anything to do with Lilah's inviting you here today."

Her heart started the hard, sickening thud it always did when he brought up anything personal between them. "I know. If I thought you had, I wouldn't have come."

He frowned at her. "Do you go around lying to yourself all the time, or do you just do it around me?"

Jenny vaulted from the couch and walked over to an old upright piano. Photos were sitting on the closed lid. She picked up one that had been taken when Lilah was in her late teens or early twenties. A smiling man in an air force uniform had his arm slung lovingly around her shoulder.

She continued to look at the pair of young lovers while her heart ached with sad regret. "I came today because of Lilah," she said, her throat tight.

"Oh, well, sure, I should have known that," he said, his voice suddenly dripping with sarcasm. "I mean, you two are such old bosom buddies, you naturally couldn't turn down her invitation."

Anger spurted through Jenny, and she whirled away from the piano to face him. "No! I couldn't turn her down. I was touched that she didn't want me spending the holiday alone. So what's your problem? Do you wish I'd stayed home? Is that what you're trying to tell me?"

He pushed himself up from the couch. In two strides he was by her side, his thumb and forefinger drawing her face to his. "I'm not trying to tell you anything of the sort! I'm trying to get you to admit you wanted to see me again. Why can't you?''

She'd been crazy to come here, Jenny thought. She'd been deluding herself to think she could be around Lucas, even for one minute, and remain indifferent to him.

"Because it . . . isn't right. Nor wise."

His dark brown eyes grew even darker as he studied her face. "It's always wise to be honest with yourself, Jenny."

"You think I'm not?"

For an answer, Lucas bent his head and gave her a hot, lingering kiss.

"Maybe that will help you make up your mind," he murmured, his lips hovering just above hers.

Jenny drew in a deep breath, and with it the clean, masculine scent of him. Her senses were reeling. That was something she couldn't deny to him or herself. He made her want him and all the things she'd never had, like a real family.

But once Jenny had finally gotten a divorce from Marcus, she'd taken a vow to remain a free woman. She was never going to let herself be hurt by another man. She had to remember that. No matter how much Lucas made her want him.

Stepping away, she turned her back on him and closed her eyes. "You must like fighting losing battles," she said her voice gruff with lingering desire.

Behind her, Lucas laughed softly. "Oh, I'm not losing, Jenny. In the next few days you're going to wake up and realize that. I always get what I want. And I want *you*."

He might want her, Jenny thought, tears stinging her eyelids. But he would never have her.

In the next few days she was going to have to wake him up and make him see that. Or they were both going to lose.

Chapter Eight

Lilah looked like a woman who'd spent most of her day in a beauty salon rather than a kitchen. But after one bite of her corn-bread dressing, Jenny was thoroughly impressed with the older woman's cooking skills.

"Lilah, this is absolutely delicious. Working as Lucas's secretary didn't teach you how to cook like this."

Obviously pleased with Jenny's praise, Lilah moved her ringed hand up to pat her carefully coiffured hair.

"Working for Lucas has taught me about patience. My mother, God rest her, taught me how to cook. You know, Jenny, back when I was very young, us girls were reared to be wives and mothers. That was our destined career. Fifty years ago, I would have never dreamed I'd wind up being a secretary instead of a wife and grandmother."

Jenny hadn't always thought of herself as being only a policewoman, either. But that's the way things had turned out.

"You were never married, Lilah?"

"Oh, yes, my dear. I was married once. John was the most exciting man I'd ever met. Still is."

Jenny glanced across the candlelit table at Lucas. She'd have to say he was the most exciting, sexy man she'd ever encountered. In fact, that last kiss was still sizzling the ends of her toes.

"The airman you were looking at in the photo with Lilah was her husband, John," he told Jenny.

"Oh, yes, I remember the photo."

"That picture was taken in 1943," Lilah said. "We'd been married three years then. I was twenty at the time. He was twenty-five and a B-52 pilot in the air force. The next year, he was killed in a bombing mission over Germany."

"How sad," Jenny said.

Lilah smiled and shook her head. "I don't like to think of it as sad, Jenny. He was my one true love, and we got to share four years with each other. That's much more than most people ever have in their lives."

"Lilah's never remarried because she can't find anyone to equal John," Lucas told Jenny, then grinned at Lilah. "But you aren't afraid to look, are you, Lilah?"

The older woman laughed at Lucas's question. "Of course I'm not afraid to look. John's death taught me to live life to the fullest, and I intend to follow that philosophy."

Lucas darted a look at Jenny. Her ex-husband wasn't dead. But she was allowing the trauma he'd put her through to jade her outlook on life. "It's too bad we can't all live by that philosophy. This world would be a happier place."

Jenny stared at the cut glass goblet in front of her plate and wished she could tell Lilah that her own husband hadn't died. Jenny herself was the one who had died during their short marriage. Like a rose battered by the elements, she'd lost the beauty of life.

"Now, Lucas," Lilah spoke up. "Each of us is different. Not everyone jumps straight into things like we do. Some of us had rather experience a little candlelight before jumping straight into the fire."

Jenny glanced at the older woman. Did she know that Lucas wanted to marry her? Darn it, Jenny thought as she stabbed her fork into a candied sweet potato, it didn't matter what Lilah knew or what philosophy she lived by. Jenny wasn't going to jump into the fire with Lucas. She wasn't going to share any candlelight with him, either.

In spite of her constant awareness of Lucas, Jenny enjoyed the Thanksgiving meal. Lilah was entertaining, to say the least, and the food was mouth-watering. Especially to Jenny, whose job forced her to eat large doses of microwaved and fast food.

After the three of them had dessert and coffee in the living room, Lilah agreed to let Jenny help her clean up the mess. She was drying the last of the pots and pans when Lucas sauntered into the cozy kitchen.

Whipping the tea towel from Jenny's hand, he began drying a large roasting pan. "Well, Oklahoma is a touchdown behind and there's three minutes to go in the fourth quarter. I don't know whether the Sooners can pull it off or not."

Lilah gave a dismissive wave of her hand. "Football! That is the most ridiculous sport. All I see is twelve men jumping on the other twelve to make a big pile. Now boxing, that's a real man's sport."

"Eleven men, Lilah. Not twelve." He looked at Jenny and winked. "Lilah loves boxing. She was ringside when Oklahoma's own Tommy Morrison punched out Big

George Foreman for the heavyweight title. That year my bonus to her was a ticket to the fight. She chose it over a week in Hawaii.''

"Well," Lilah said with a sniff, "Hawaii is there to see anytime. I wanted to see the main event."

Lucas put the roasting pan on the counter and tossed the tea towel inside it.

"Speaking of seeing things," Lucas told the older woman, "I want to show Jenny the downtown shelter. Would you mind if we ate and ran?"

Lilah patted his arm. "Go on. I get an eyeful of you every day. You take Jenny and show her what good work you've been doing. Even though it is killing you," she added.

Jenny stared at the two of them. She didn't want to go anywhere with Lucas! She'd already spent more time with him today than she'd intended. But how could she refuse to go while Lilah was looking on like a proud mother?

"I really should be getting home, Lucas," Jenny told him. "I've got a long day ahead of me tomorrow."

"You can follow me in your car. That will save the time of driving back to get it. And I promise not to keep you out past midnight."

The look he was giving her was devilish and daunting. Jenny was suddenly reminded of Lilah's words about jumping straight into the fire. "Okay, I'll take a look at the shelter. But only for a few minutes."

Ignoring the victorious little smile on Lucas's face, Jenny went over to Lilah and kissed the woman's smooth cheek. "Thank you for such a lovely meal, Lilah. I hope you'll let me fix dinner for you sometime. I don't have a whole lot of cooking skills, but I can put on a pretty good feed when I try."

Lilah hugged Jenny's shoulder. "I'll be there."

The two women exchanged goodbyes, then Lucas took Jenny by the elbow and urged her out of the kitchen.

"You know," Jenny said as the two of them walked down the drive to their parked vehicles, "every time I get around you, I end up doing things I never intended to do."

Laughing, Lucas opened the car door for her. "And every time I get around you I don't get to do nearly half of what I want to do."

Thank goodness, Jenny thought, as she slid onto the car seat. Lucas shut the door, then with a little wave went to his own vehicle. Jenny backed out onto the street and waited for him to take the lead.

Since it was a quiet holiday afternoon, traffic was practically nonexistent, allowing them to make the trip to the shelter in less than five minutes. Jenny parked behind Lucas, then waited out on the sidewalk while he unlocked the front entrance.

"This place isn't far from your business," Jenny remarked as the two of them stepped inside the building.

"Three blocks," he said. "I used to store tires and truck parts in here."

"Well, it certainly doesn't look like a warehouse now," Jenny said as she gazed around the large, family-type room.

He walked over to where she was standing, and Jenny rested her eyes on his face. "I know this is probably boring to you," he said, "all this kid stuff that I do with my extra time and money. Back at Lilah's it was pretty obvious you didn't want to come here."

She took a deep breath and tried not to notice how good he looked. Not that there was anything different about him today. He wasn't wearing anything special. Just a long-sleeved white shirt with a pair of blue jeans and black roper boots. He didn't have on a belt or any sort of jewelry or accessory to add spark to his appearance. But then Lucas hardly needed help in that department, she thought. One little grin on his face was like the flash of a thousand diamonds.

"Nothing about children bores me, Lucas. And I think what you're doing here is—well, it's far above admirable. But I..."

A wry smile on his mouth, he moved a step closer and lifted her hand in his. "You just don't want to be around me any more than you have to."

He said it as a statement rather than a question, as though he knew exactly what was going on in her mind. A few minutes ago, Jenny would have hastily agreed with him. But now, as she looked at him, she knew that wasn't quite true. She did like to be with Lucas. In fact, when she was with him she felt more alive, more like a woman than she ever had in her entire life. But on the other hand, she was desperately afraid of him. Without any effort at all he could tear her scarred heart into tiny little shreds.

"I only said no to your proposal, Lucas. I didn't tell you I disliked you."

A slow grin spread across his face and he swiped a hand across his brow. "Whew! I'm glad to know I haven't been kissing a woman who didn't like me. As for the marrying part, well, that's still under negotiation. I want you for my wife."

"Only in your dreams," she told him.

Still grinning, he took her by the arm and led her out of the room. "Don't count on it, my sweet Jenny. I used to act as a mediator for the trucker's union. I can be powerfully persuasive when I want to be."

No doubt he'd swayed many minds in the boardroom. But Jenny figured his powers of persuasion would be far greater in the bedroom.

"You've been a lot of things, Lucas. A marine, a truck driver, a successful businessman. But you haven't been a husband."

They entered a long corridor where separate sleeping units had been built. Lucas opened the door of the first room and ushered Jenny in. She was immediately struck by the bright, happy colors.

"You're right. I haven't been a husband. But I'm working to change that," he pointed out.

Desperate to put space between them, Jenny began to move around the small room. When she reached the foot of the single bed, her hand smoothed over the shiny red metal railing. "You're thirty-five years old," she told him. "You're used to doing what you want, when you want. You might not like having to accommodate a wife's wishes."

Lucas's eyes traveled slowly over her. He didn't know whether it was the sensual curves of her body, the bright flaming crown of hair or the toughness of her voice that had attracted him the first day he'd met her. Whatever it was, that attraction had grown tenfold. His feelings for her had grown even more. He loved her. It was that simple. Yet when he saw that stubborn resistance on her face as it was at this moment, he knew nothing about their relationship was simple.

"I think the accommodating would be very easy—if you were my wife."

Her eyes jerked to his, and Lucas could see that just the idea of them being intimately linked was enough to shake her.

"I hardly think so, Lucas. My work schedule constantly changes. I'm called out in the middle of the night, on holidays or anytime I'm needed. You think that would be easy to deal with?"

"You don't have to remind me of your job, Jenny. I haven't forgotten, even for one minute, that you're a policewoman. But I love you and I've come to the decision that I'm not going to let your career become an issue between us. You're a policewoman and your job is important to you. I'd never ask or expect you to give it up for me."

He was getting too personal, too generous and understanding for Jenny's peace of mind. She refused to believe that any man could love her *that* much.

"I didn't come here to talk about marriage. I don't want to talk about it."

Frustrated, Lucas threw his hands helplessly up in the air. "Then talk to me about something else. What do you think about the room? They're all pretty much like this one."

How could she think about the room when his presence was filling every inch of it? "I think any child would enjoy making this room his or her own private little space."

"Good."

When he didn't say more, Jenny nervously licked her lips, then darted a glance at him. "So now what?"

He gave a negligible little shrug as though he didn't care what happened next. Yet Jenny could see tension in his stance, in the corded muscles on his neck and jaw.

"We could go look at the kitchen and dining room," he said. But rather than make a move to leave the room, he continued to stand where he was, his eyes locked on her face.

Jenny's heart lurched into an erratic gallop. "Is that what you want?"

Maybe it was the phrasing of her question, or maybe it was the hunger inside him that suddenly compelled Lucas to close the small gap between them and bare his true wants to her.

"Where you're concerned, Jenny Prescott, I have several wants. The most immediate one is to make love to you."

Even though that very thing had been consuming her mind, she hadn't expected him to come out and say it so bluntly. The fact that he had sent a tingling rush through her body.

Seconds passed as Lucas's face hovered just above hers. His brown eyes probed deeply into her green ones. Jenny's ears began to roar as though she was going to faint. Fearing her knees would betray her, she reached out and grabbed the front of his white shirt.

"That wasn't very subtle," she finally murmured.

The hint of a dimple appeared in his cheek. As Jenny watched his eyelids droop, her heart began to pound harder and harder. Heat pooled deep within her and sent flames of color to her face.

"You're a cop," he said. "You don't sugarcoat anything. Why should I?" His hands came up to gently frame her face. "Besides, we both know we've been skirting around the issue for a long time now."

Unknowingly, her hands relaxed their grip on his shirt and flattened against his chest. He felt warm and hard and so wonderfully masculine. She moved her hands ever so slightly against him.

"The issue being?" she asked, her voice a soft invitation.

Groaning, he pulled her into his arms. "This, among other things," he said roughly, then fastened his mouth over hers.

At the moment Jenny was too mesmerized to resist him. She opened her mouth and met the swift invasion of his tongue against hers.

Lucas wrapped his arms around her waist and hugged her tightly against him. Jenny's hands slid around his back, then moved upward to anchor a grip on both his shoulders.

As his lips hungrily fed on hers, his tongue continued to explore the ribbed roof of her mouth and the sharp edge of her teeth. In response, Jenny bit and nibbled and tasted the sweet mystery of him.

It was anything but a gentle kiss. It was hungry and hot and so consuming that Jenny felt totally drugged by the time Lucas lifted his head and his breath fanned against her cheeks.

"Tell me you didn't like that," he dared beneath a ragged breath.

"I did like it."

"Tell me you don't want me," he persisted.

Her eyelids fluttered open, and she groaned at the sight of his lips only a fraction away from hers. "I do want you, Lucas. I don't want to. But I do."

He looked at her, his eyes full of wonder and love, then he lifted her into his arms and carried her to the narrow bed.

He lay her on the mattress, then followed her down, his lips once again locked onto hers. Jenny didn't protest. She couldn't. It had been a long time since she'd been the focus of a man's desire. And even longer still since she'd felt desire herself. This man wanted her. And she wanted him. For the moment that was all she could think about.

With their bodies crushed together, Lucas wedged his fingers to the front of her sweater and began to push the tiny buttons through their buttonholes. Inch by inch, the pale pink sweater began to part until her naked breasts were exposed to him.

The fact that she wasn't wearing a bra only added to Lucas's conviction that he'd been right about Jenny all along. She wasn't cold and dispassionate, as she believed. Beneath those cool blue uniforms she wore was a warm-blooded woman.

"Oh, Jenny, this is the way it should be between us," he murmured, his head dipping to the sweet swell of her breast. "For now and always."

How could Jenny argue when it felt so right, so exquisitely perfect to have him touching her, loving her this way?

Closing her eyes, she sighed as Lucas's hands cupped the firm weight of her breast. His lips made a warm, moist trail around each budded nipple. Eventually, his teeth clamped gently over one hard peak. Fire shot through Jenny and her body arched against his, silently begging him to ease the ache he was building inside her.

Lucas's hands slid beneath her skirt, up the silken softness of her thighs, then gripped her hips and tugged them against his. By then Jenny was panting, her head reeling with the raw desire to make love to him.

After a moment Lucas spoke against her cheek. "This is the way it's going to be, Jenny. We're going to be husband and wife. We're going to make love and have children. We're going to be happy. So happy."

Happy? As he kissed her again, the word whirled around in Jenny's head like a strange mantra that frightened rather than soothed. She didn't know what it was to be truly happy. And she'd be deluding him and herself if she believed she could be a happily-ever-after wife and mother.

Twisting her lips away from his, she pushed at his shoulders. Lucas immediately rolled off her. Snatching the edges of her sweater together, Jenny sat up and flung her hair out of her eyes.

"This is wrong, Lucas," she gasped breathlessly.

His brow puckered as he took in her heaving breasts and pink lips. "Wrong? It felt damn right to me."

She wiggled her way to the edge of the bed and swung her legs over the side. "Yes," she murmured, painfully. "It felt right. But feelings aren't enough for me."

Desire was squeezing Lucas's insides like a hot, heavy hand. He wanted to make love to her, show her how wonderful it could be between them. Yet here she was telling him that feelings weren't enough for her. He wanted to ram his fist through the wall.

"What the hell is enough, Jenny? Don't human wants and needs ever figure in your life? Or have you been a cop for so long you have to have cold hard facts to satisfy you?"

Glaring at him, she slid off the bed and looked around for her shoes, which had fallen off when he'd lifted her onto the bed. "That's a rotten thing to say!"

"Rotten, but true, I think."

Her teeth grinding together, she jabbed her feet into the black flats. "I don't have to listen to this!"

Lucas rose from the bed. His eyes glinted like ice as they traveled over her angry face. "No," he said, "you don't have to listen to me, or make love to me. Marry me, have my children, or do any damn thing with me! You can go home by yourself and tomorrow you can strap on your revolver, pin on your badge and pretend that's all you want out of life."

Rage sizzled through her like a bolt of hot lightning. She flew at him instantly, and before she realized what she was about to do, her fist cracked solidly against his jaw.

Lucas remained stock-still, his face a rigid mask. Horrified, Jenny stared at him while her whole body began to shake.

What had come over her? Dear God, what sort of woman had she turned into?

Lifting her hand to his face, Jenny gently touched his reddening cheek. "Lucas, I'm—I'm so sorry," she whispered with remorse. "I didn't—I never meant to hurt you. I—"

Suddenly sobs were blocking her throat, making it impossible to say more. With a muffled cry, she whirled away from him and ran out of the room.

Lucas caught up to her as she was about to leave the building. Grabbing her shoulders, he spun her around, then pinned her against the door.

"Let me go!" she sobbed. "Haven't I shown you enough of me yet? Can't you see that I'm not the woman for you? I'm—I'm not worth loving!"

Tears were streaming down her face and throat and soaking into the collar of her sweater. With his palms, Lucas wiped her cheeks, then cupped her chin.

"You pack a hell of a wallop, Jenny. And I'm not just talking about your right hook. I want you more than I've ever wanted any woman in life. And I don't care if you break both my jaws and fight me till hell freezes over. You're not going to change the way I feel about you. I love you. Don't you understand? I *love* you!"

"No—you can't! I don't want you to love me!"

Desperate, Jenny wrenched away from his hold and shot through the door. Afraid he would follow, she ran down the sidewalk to her car, slid inside and quickly jabbed the key in the ignition. Once the engine started, she dared to look up.

Through a blur of hot tears she could see that the sidewalk was empty and the door to the Ray Lowrimore House remained closed. Drawing in a ragged breath of relief, Jenny jerked the car into gear and sped away from the curb.

A few blocks passed before she loosened her death grip on the steering wheel and wiped the tears from her face.

A glance in the rearview mirror assured her that Lucas wasn't coming after her. No, Jenny thought, her heart as heavy as dull lead, Lucas wouldn't come after her now. He was well and truly out of her life. And that was the way she wanted it. That was the way it was going to stay.

Chapter Nine

Jenny cried all that night. Sometime before dawn she fell into an exhausted sleep and woke a few hours later with just enough time to shower and drive to work.

Her red eyes and swollen face made her look as though she'd downed a pint of vodka, but thankfully none of her fellow officers noticed or made any comments about her appearance when she walked through the station house.

When Jenny reached her desk, she was greeted with a large woven basket of freshly cut sunflowers. The sight of the bouquet was such a shock that for a moment all she could do was sink on her desk chair and stare at the bright yellow petals.

After yesterday evening, she'd never expected to hear from Lucas again. He was a smart man. She figured he would come to the conclusion that pursuing her was heading him down a dead-end street to trouble.

"Flowers for you again," Glenda said enviously as she

paused by Jenny's workplace. "I wish I knew how you did it."

"I hardly know myself," Jenny murmured more to herself than to Glenda.

The little blond secretary motioned toward the flowers. "Aren't you going to see who they're from?"

Jenny didn't need to open the card to know who sent the flowers. There was only one man with that much persistence. Only one man who would still be thinking of her even though she'd socked him in the face. And to know that he was still thinking of her made her heart weep.

"Oh, well, you don't have to tell me," Glenda went on with an airy wave of her hand. "If the guy is that crazy about you, he's bound to show up here at the station sooner or later, and then I'll get a look for myself."

Captain Morgan's secretary swished her way down the cluttered aisle between the cramped row of desks. Once the woman was out of sight, Jenny reached for the small white envelope nestled among the flowers.

The card read, Trust me. Lucas.

Three little words. Jenny didn't know what she'd been expecting the card to say. I love you, or maybe I want to see you. Or even call me. Instead he'd simply said to trust him.

Her dry, aching eyes began to burn with tears. Quickly Jenny ducked her head and pressed her fingers hard against her closed eyelids. Her crying had to stop here and now. She was a police officer. She couldn't afford to let herself become soft and distracted. Otherwise, she might wind up getting herself or her partner killed.

Three days later, Savanna arrived at Jenny's apartment and insisted she accompany her on a shopping trip to a nearby mall. Deciding anything would be better than sitting around trying to keep her mind off Lucas, Jenny threw on some lipstick and a coat and followed her friend out the door.

The late November day was cloudy and cold. After the two women climbed into the car, Savanna switched the heater on high, then looked over and giggled at the sight of Jenny shivering inside her red coat.

"Aren't you glad Joe bought me this new car? Otherwise we'd be driving my Beetle with no heater."

"Oh, no," Jenny said between chattering teeth. "I would drive us in my car before I'd get back into that orange sardine can of yours. You drove that thing like it was a racing machine."

Savanna pretended to be insulted until a giggle finally gave her away. "Joe said the same thing. That's why he bought me this one. He says it's much safer for me."

"He wants to keep you around awhile," Jenny reasoned.

Savanna smiled as she negotiated the car out of the parking lot. "Yes, he does. So where do you want to go? Crossroads Mall or some place closer?"

"Crossroads will be fine. I don't have to be at work until eight this evening. Orville and I are pulling a late shift." The car's interior was already starting to warm up. Jenny removed her coat and tugged down the cuffs of her sweater. "Was your trip to New Orleans a good one?"

Nodding, Savanna went on to talk about the lovely time she'd had visiting her father and stepmother over the holiday.

"What did you do on Thanksgiving?" Savanna asked a few minutes later.

Jenny stared out the window at the busy interstate traffic. "I worked for part of the day. Then I had dinner with Lucas and his secretary."

"Jenny! That's great! Things must be heating up between you two."

Savanna didn't know the half of it, Jenny thought. Things had already heated up and boiled over. Other than receiving the sunflowers, she hadn't seen or talked to Lucas since Thanksgiving. But she expected to any day now. He'd been calling her at home and at the station house, leaving messages for her to contact him. So far she'd ignored them, yet she knew he wouldn't give up that easily. Sooner or later, she would look up and he'd be there. And the anticipation of facing him again kept her constantly on edge.

"Oh, by the way," Savanna went on slyly. "I saw your Lucas in the paper this morning. He's quite a hunk, Jen. He even looked good in grainy black and white. I can't imagine how he'd be in person."

Jenny's gaze jerked over to her friend. "Lucas's picture was in the paper? Is something wrong with him? Was there a story with it?"

"Calm down. There wasn't an accident or anything like that. It was something about a charity benefit for children. The way it read, Lucas Lowrimore is one of the city's leading contributors to children's projects."

"He is."

"Hm. Sounds like a generous-hearted man. Or he needs a whale of a tax write-off."

"Believe me, he doesn't do it for tax reasons. Lucas is— well, he didn't have a mother while he was growing up and he hasn't always had money. So it's easy for him to relate to a child's needs."

"You think Lucas would make a good father?"

Like a heavy cape, sadness settled around her shoulders. "Lucas would make a warm, loving father."

Savanna made an impatient sound in her throat. "You're singing his praises, Jenny, yet I can hear a big but in your voice."

Jenny sighed heavily. "Savanna, I didn't come out with you today to discuss my interest, or lack of it, in Lucas Lowrimore."

Savanna shrugged. "That's too bad. Because you're going to discuss it whether you want to or not."

Jenny rolled her eyes helplessly. No matter what spewed out of Savanna's mouth, she couldn't get mad at her. And the other woman knew it.

"The situation with me is still the same, Savanna," Jenny said with exaggerated patience. "I don't think marrying Lucas, or any man for that matter, would be the right thing for me to do."

Groaning with disbelief, Savanna shook her head. "Jenny, I hardly think a man with that sort of love and compassion for children would start knocking you around after you were married."

Jenny stared at her lap. Images of Lucas and his farmhouse floated into her mind. He would do more than make the rooms beautiful with carpentry work, he would eventually turn the place into a real home. Someday he would find that woman he'd been searching for and they would make love in the very room where Jenny had stood close beside him, touched him and listened as he told her about his mother.

Knowing she couldn't be *that* woman was a constant torture to her, and she was beginning to wonder how much longer it was going to be before she finally cracked into emotional pieces.

"No. I don't think Lucas could ever be abusive, either," she said after a moment. "But let's face it, Savanna, I'm not wife material. After the glow of the honeymoon wore off, I think Lucas would be disenchanted with me. Especially with me working the streets every day as a law enforcer."

Savanna cast a keen glance at Jenny. "Have you ever thought about giving up your job?"

Jenny leaned her head back against the car seat and closed her eyes. "My job is my life. It's all I am and all I know. Why would I want to give it all up for Lucas?"

Savanna smiled and tapped a rhythmic beat on the steering wheel. "Because he's probably worth it. And because you've had ten years of law work. Maybe it's time you chose a different life for yourself."

"That's easy for you to say. Your life is all settled. You have a good husband, an adorable stepdaughter and a child on the way. You're looking at the world through happy eyes."

"Don't you think it's time you looked at the world through happy eyes, too?" Savanna countered.

With a slow shake of her head, Jenny turned her gaze out the window. Right now the only thing she could see was tears.

At four o'clock the next morning, Jenny wrote out the last of her arrest reports, then carefully placed them in manila folders. The night had been a long one for her and Orville. The two of them had made several arrests and chased down a stolen car. The driver had turned out to be a fugitive wanted by the law in several states.

Normally, Jenny enjoyed a shift that had more than just routine traffic stops to keep them busy. But tonight she was bone tired. Even praise from her captain on apprehending the wanted fugitive hadn't lifted her heavy spirits.

Have you ever thought about quitting your job?

Savanna's words fluttered tauntingly through her mind. Of course she'd thought of retiring after she'd put in twenty years of service. She'd always planned to train to be a counselor for abused women once her stint as a police officer was over. Even so, she'd never thought of giving up being a cop before that time arrived. That is, until Lucas had come along and dallied with her mind.

Now she was asking herself if quitting her job and marrying Lucas would make her a happy woman. Being a police officer was the only good thing she'd ever had in her life. During her horrendous marriage to Marcus, it had been her sole salvation to know that at least for a few hours each day she could go to a job where no man would dare try to intimidate her. It had made her feel safe to be a policewoman back then, and it still did today. And, to Jenny, being safe was the most important thing of all.

She couldn't give that up for Lucas. She wouldn't give it up for any man.

Rising from her desk, she carried the reports to the filing room. As she placed the last folder in its proper alphabetical order, she thought of the long arrest record they'd discovered on the fugitive she and Orville had caught tonight. Years ago it would have taken hours, even days to collect that much information on a suspect. Now all a police officer had to do was type a name into a computer.

Where is Marcus now? Lucas's question hit her like a hammer. Could her ex-husband actually be in prison, or had her answer been just wishful thinking on her part? If Marcus had gotten into any sort of trouble with the law, she could easily find him in the computer bank.

Moments later, at her desk, she quickly read the information beneath Marcus's name and social security number. Her suspicions had been right! He was doing time in the McAlester State Penitentiary for theft and assault with intent to kill.

Leaning back in her chair, Jenny switched off the computer and let out a long sigh. She was relieved that Marcus could no longer harm her or any other woman. She'd often felt guilty because she'd never pressed charges against him. And she'd fervently prayed these past few years that he wouldn't inflict his abuse on someone else. Now she didn't have to worry about that anymore. Marcus was behind bars and would be there for a long time.

Yet the whole thing left her wondering how she could have loved and married a man with such a black, violent nature. He'd gone from bad to worse. Why hadn't she been able to see that, all those years ago, before she'd ever become his wife? Was she that gullible where men and love were concerned? Was her judgment too poor to be trusted?

Thrusting the troubling questions aside, Jenny left her desk, then went to the locker room for her purse and duffel bag. It was time to go home and try to get a few hours of rest.

Sunrise was still a good three hours away, and a cloudy sky made the early morning seem that much darker as she made her way across the parking lot to her waiting car.

"Hello, Jenny."

She was unlocking the car door when Lucas's voice sounded right behind her shoulder. Jenny's already strained nerves bolted, making her head jerk. The car keys fell to the cold asphalt.

"Damn it, what are you doing sneaking up on me like that?" she gasped.

He bent over and picked up her keys, then handed them to her.

"I wasn't sneaking. You weren't paying attention. A mugger could have been behind you and you would have never known it."

Annoyed because he was right, she turned her back to him and jabbed the key into the car door. "I hardly think a mugger would be loitering around a police station parking lot."

"No, just a seedy-eyed stalker like me."

Not bothering to open the door, she twisted around to him. "I didn't say that."

He grimaced. "You might as well have."

"Did you come here to pick a fight?"

Rather than grab her and pull her into his arms like he wanted to do, Lucas jammed his fists into the pockets of his leather jacket. "I think you know why I'm here. I've tried to call you for the past several days. You've always been out. I left messages for you to return my calls. Why didn't you?"

Jenny had known he would show up sooner or later. Even so, she wasn't prepared for what the sight of him was doing to her. She felt shaky, weak and vulnerable. She loved this man, there was no point in denying it. And everything inside her wanted to fling her arms around his neck and never let go. But fear in the form of dark painful memories, held her back.

"I thought it best not to."

"You thought it best," he said, his voice edged with sarcasm. "Best for you? For me? Or have you ever stopped thinking about yourself long enough to consider my feelings?"

Anger ripped through her, then just as quickly vanished. Had she only been thinking of her own wants and needs without any regard to Lucas? She didn't want to think so. "If it seems that way, I'm sorry. It's just because I can see things as they really are."

"You can?" he asked dryly.

She looked at him, her face pinched with cold and pain, her eyes begging him to understand. "I don't know why, but when you look at me, Lucas, it's through a pair of rose-colored glasses. There's nothing wonderful or special about me. I'm just a woman with a damaged heart and I can't make it whole again no matter how much you want me to."

Lucas's somber gaze took in the gaunt, haunted shadows on her face. He could see he was hurting her. It was the last thing he wanted to do. Yet he couldn't just give up and walk away from her. Good or bad, she was in his heart. And she was there to stay.

He stepped closer, slid his hand inside her bomber jacket and touched her breast and the cold metal badge pinned above it.

"Your heart isn't damaged, Jenny. You only think it is. The other night I felt it beating for me. I know you love me. You just don't want to say it."

The tears she'd struggled with all week were threatening to fill her eyes. "And what if I did say it, Lucas? It wouldn't change anything. I still won't marry you."

After Lucas had left the marines, he'd lost his quick temper and the sudden urge to use his fists. But he hadn't lost his will to fight until he won.

Reaching around her, he opened the car door, pushed Jenny inside, then slid in after her.

"What are you doing?" she demanded when he slammed the door and the two of them were confined inside the small car.

"This."

Suddenly she was crushed in the circle of his arms and her lips were captured beneath his. In the back of Jenny's mind she knew she should push him away. She even told herself to do it. But her body refused to obey her brain's command.

Instead her lips clung to his, her hands curved around the warm muscles of his neck and the solid ridge of his jaw. He made her feel alive, wanted and, most of all, loved. And that very thing was what terrified Jenny the most.

Love made people vulnerable. It opened them up and left the door to their hearts wide open so that any sort of pain could walk inside. Loving Marcus had not only hurt Jenny, it had gotten her into a dangerous situation. What would loving Lucas to do her?

"Say it, Jenny," he whispered huskily. "Say you love me."

His lips finally breaking free of hers, he planted kisses across her cheeks, her eyes, her nose and forehead. And every battle that Jenny had fought with herself over Lucas this past week now seemed in vain. With one kiss he could touch her, melt her down to a piece of gooey chocolate begging to be eaten.

"All right, Lucas. I love you."

The admission was a painful relief to Jenny. Yet the look on Lucas's face said the heavens had just opened up and it was raining drops of pure joy.

"Oh, Jenny, my darling." He groaned against her cheek. "You don't know what it means to me to hear you say you love me. I—"

Before he could go any farther, Jenny wriggled out of his embrace and huddled against the passenger door.

"It doesn't matter, Lucas," she said in a strained voice. "I'm not going to marry you."

"Jenny—"

He reached for her, but Jenny quickly warded him off. If she didn't make a stand now, she knew the whole battle would be over.

Her lips quivering, she said, "I don't want to see you anymore, Lucas. I don't want you to call me. I don't want you to come to my apartment. I don't want you to try to contact me again. Ever!"

The conviction in her voice tore a hole right through Lucas. Until that moment, he'd never known that loving someone could hurt so badly.

"And what if I do?" he asked quietly.

What would she do? More than likely she'd break down and give in to him. He would eventually persuade her to marry him and then they'd both suffer the consequences.

Jenny drew in a breath of cold air and tried to find the courage to look at him. But her eyes could get no closer than the top button of his shirt.

"If I have to, I'll get a restraining order against you."

Lucas suddenly felt cold to the bone. "You'd do that to me?"

Of course Jenny wouldn't. But for both their sakes she had to make Lucas believe her. She nodded. "If I have to."

Lucas shook his head. "There haven't been many times in my life that I've been taken for a fool. But I have to admit, you've done a good job of it." His eyes leveled accusingly on her face. "I thought you were a woman who'd weathered a storm and come out stronger because of it."

Jenny was certain that what little there was left of her heart was dying right here and now. "Well, you must be very glad you uncovered the real Jenny Prescott before you made the fatal mistake of marrying me."

"Oh, I'm damn glad," he sneered. "Don't you see me laughing?"

"I know you don't understand me," she said, her voice wobbling. "But I'm doing this because I love you. I want you to be happy."

He made a snorting sound of disbelief. "And what about you, Jenny? Don't you want to be happy, or will getting away from me do that for you?"

Marcus had used his fist to pound her self-worth down to nothing. These past five years Jenny had worked to get it back, and she believed she had, until Lucas had come into her life.

"It's—it's too late for me, Lucas. Someday you'll look back and understand that."

"No! That day will never come, Jenny. You're the one who's going to have to wake up and take a good hard look around you. I know you've been knocked around in your life. Literally and figuratively. But I shouldn't have to pay for some other man's slimy behavior. I love you. I'm offering you a lifetime of happiness. But you don't want it. You'd rather wallow around in self-pity and pretend your life is over."

Inside Jenny, anger flared like a kerosene torch. "How dare you say that! I've never wanted pity from anyone, including myself. And until you badgered your way into my life, I was fine. Just fine and dandy!"

Lucas reached behind him and tripped the door latch. "Well, you've got nothing to worry about now, Officer Prescott. You won't ever be seeing me again!" He opened the door and climbed out. Then, sticking his head into the car, he added, "Unless I see you in traffic court. And I'll warn you right now, I wouldn't pay without a fight."

"Get out!"

"Goodbye, Jenny."

He slammed the door and Jenny slumped weakly against the seat. In the parking slot next to her, Lucas's pickup fired to life, then pulled away.

She'd finally done it. He was out of her life. There would be no more phone calls, invitations to go out with him or flowers on her desk. There would be no more kisses to melt her bones. No more temptations, no more worry that she might be human enough to give in to him.

Suddenly her teeth began to chatter and her body shook. It was a cold night, but Jenny knew it wasn't the weather that had given her a violent case of the shivers. It was her frozen heart.

Dragging herself behind the steering wheel, Jenny started the engine then headed the car toward her apartment. In a couple of hours dawn would break and fingers of gray light would streak the night sky.

Normally after Jenny pulled a late shift, she'd sit in her little kitchen, drink her morning coffee and watch the sun rise over the city. But this morning, Jenny didn't think the sun would ever shine on her again.

Chapter Ten

"I can have your beef out to Sacramento in three days. No more. No less. If you can find another trucking company that can beat that time, then more power to you, Mr. Varnum. But I'll not push my drivers any harder than that. Their safety and the safety of others on the highway comes first with me. I know—"

Lucas looked up to see Lilah standing inside the door. She was obviously waiting for him to get off the phone, and Lucas was more than glad for a reason to end the conversation. "Okay, Varnum, get Red River to move your product, but don't come whining to me when the wholesaler tells you he has a truckload of green T-bone steaks on his hands!"

He slammed the phone on its hook, then tossed his pen toward a metal holder. It missed and clattered to the floor. Lilah immediately walked over and picked up the expensive writing instrument.

Casting him a disapproving look, she said, "I was going to show you something. But I'm not so sure you're ready for it."

With a tired sigh, Lucas leaned back in his seat and raked both hands over his sleek black hair. "If it's about that transmission Frank ordered for truck forty-three, tell them it had better be here by Friday morning or they'll not be selling it to me!"

The line of Lilah's lips grew thinner. "It's nothing about the transmission. That will be here tomorrow."

"Thank God. I've had enough problems this past week without adding that one to the list."

Lilah put the pen in its rightful place on his desk, then picked up several foam cups partially filled with leftover coffee. "You know, Mr. Lowrimore, from the time you started this business you've had plenty of problems every day of the week. And no matter how bad they got, you never let them get you down. So why are you now?"

The old adage that you could never judge anything by its outward appearance more than proved itself when Lucas looked at his secretary. She was an outrageous throwback from the sixties, but she was also one of the shrewdest people he'd ever known.

"I guess it's like I told you before, Lilah. I'm starting to feel my age."

She let out an unladylike snort. "Old! When you get to be my age, you might use that excuse and get by with it. But for right now, it's pretty obvious you have something on your mind. And I'm beginning to wonder if Jenny Prescott has anything to do with it."

Restless, Lucas rose to his feet and walked to the window overlooking the yard. "Jenny and I are no more. Not that we ever were," he added caustically.

Lilah studied his pensive profile. "What happened?"

The question unleashed a torrent of emotions roiling through Lucas. He threw up both hands in frustrated surrender. "The woman has a mental problem."

"She seems perfectly sane and intelligent to me."

"I don't mean like that! She has—well, maybe I should have said emotional problems. She lets them rule her head."

Lilah suddenly laughed. "All women do that, Lucas. Otherwise, we'd behave just like you men. And if you ask me, that would make the world a very boring place."

Lucas absently rubbed the pads of his fingers over the five o'clock shadow on his jaws. "She doesn't want to marry me."

"Why not?"

A tight grimace on his face, Lucas continued to look out over the fleet of tractor-trailer rigs marked with his initials. Normally the sight of the trucks gave him a proud sense of achievement. Today they meant nothing to him.

Twisting away from the window, Lucas stalked to his desk where Lilah was still hanging on to the dirty coffee cups.

"She was married once before. And the marriage was bad. Really bad. Her husband abused her."

"Bastard."

Lucas couldn't have said it better. "She says the marriage ruined her and she believes she wouldn't make a good wife for me. But damn, Lilah, I think she's just afraid of me."

Lilah rolled her eyes at him, then swished over to the trash basket and tossed in the cups. "Lucas, any normal woman in her right mind would be afraid to make a commitment to a man after she'd been through such a thing. I surely would be. And I love men!"

Any other time Lilah's last statement would have put a smile on Lucas's face. But not today.

"Anyway," the secretary went on, "she isn't afraid of you. She's afraid of what you represent. Don't you understand that?"

"I understand that she's treating me as if I'm just as much of a snake as he was. Each time I tried to get close to her, she ran away."

"Did you ever think you might be rushing her? After all, Lucas, you haven't known her all that long."

Lucas paced across the room, then back to his desk. "Maybe I did come on strong," he admitted. "But I wasn't pushing her to set a wedding date! Aw, hell, it doesn't matter anyway. She never wants to see me again. And I'm glad to oblige her."

"You look like you're glad," Lilah said with obvious sarcasm.

Lucas shot her a dry glare. "I'm not only glad, I'm relieved. She saved me from making the same mistake my father made. Marrying a woman too weak to stand under pressure."

Lilah muttered a curse word that Lucas had never heard her use before. "If you think that about Jenny, then she's better off without you!"

The older woman walked to the door, then paused with her hand on the knob. "Don't bother coming out to look at the Christmas tree I just decorated. You wouldn't appreciate it anyway."

"Christmas tree!" he shouted. "Hell, Lilah, it isn't even December yet!"

She peered at him over the rims of her rhinestone-studded glasses. "Sorry, Lucas, but it's been December for five days now."

Dumbfounded, Lucas watched his secretary close the door behind her. He hadn't even realized it was December! Had his thoughts been that consumed with Jenny?

Yes! She was in his mind every moment of every day. He missed her. And though he'd vowed to put her out of his life, Lucas couldn't seem to push her out of his thoughts. He kept envisioning her in the farmhouse, the pleasure he'd seen in her eyes as she walked through the rooms, the wistful look on her face when he'd talked about having children.

Even though he'd made an angry vow to comply with her wishes to stay away, this past week he'd found himself wanting to pick up the phone and dial her number. More than twice he'd found himself driving toward her apartment, only to turn back before he reached it. Lucas didn't know why he wanted her so. She'd done her best to spurn him, and a man's ego could only take so much rejection. But even the fact that she threatened to get a restraining order against him hadn't quelled his love for her.

His heart was totally and irrevocably lost to her. So what was he going to do about it?

Puffing heavily, Jenny lugged the ten-speed bicycle through the door of her apartment, then after pausing for a few needed breaths, she rolled it into the bedroom and rested it in an out-of-the-way spot.

She'd ridden five miles this morning. Normally that distance was a breeze for her, but today her lungs were burning and her legs felt like two wet noodles.

She was out of shape, she thought disgustedly. For the past month she'd been lax about exercising. Usually she made a point of either riding her bike or working out at the gym. But ever since Lucas had entered upon the scene, it seemed her schedule had ceased to exist.

She didn't know why. She hadn't spent that much time with the man. *But what time you weren't with the man, you were thinking about him. And you're still thinking about him.*

Wearily, she tugged a hooded sweatshirt over her head, used it to wipe the perspiration from her face, then tossed it in a nearby hamper.

It had been a week since Lucas had walked up on her in the police station parking lot. Jenny had never gone through such a miserable seven days in her life.

She'd believed that once she cut all ties with Lucas and was away from him long enough to step back and take a hard look at things, she'd be able to see how right she'd been to end their relationship.

Well, these past few days, she'd done her best to step back and look. She'd tried to see the rightness of her decision to stay out of his life, but her heart kept getting in the way.

Jenny had always believed her job would remain the most important thing in her life. She'd always thought being a policewoman would be enough for her. But this past week, her job had been more like drudgery than salvation. She'd worked her shifts automatically, relying on years of habit to get her through. She'd made no mistakes. But the luster and enjoyment were gone, and Jenny seriously doubted they would ever return.

She walked to the dresser, leaned toward the mirror and peered closely at her face. Jenny had never been a vain person. Other than when she was dabbing on a little makeup, she rarely ever looked in the mirror. Certainly, she'd never thought of herself as beautiful or desirable. After Marcus, those things had ceased to be important to her.

Her fingertips lightly traced the fine lines at the corners of her eyes and mouth, the pale freckles across her nose. Lucas had kissed her face, touched it as though it was lovelier than a summer sunset.

Stepping back, she looked at the shape of her body outlined by a pair of Lycra exercise pants and tank top. She was still slender, her biological clock still ticking at an orderly pace.

Jenny had long ago ceased to think of herself as a mother. But loving Lucas had made all those maternal longings come back to her. Could she be a mother? If she laid down her badge and gun and quit working the streets, would she have the right amount of softness and tenderness to nurture a baby?

Her hands drifted down to rest against her lower belly. What would it be like to have Lucas's baby growing inside her? How would it feel to finally hold their child in her arms and know they had created it out of love?

Love! Damn, Jenny, you loved Marcus once, too. Look what that got you. There were no babies or happily ever after!

Disgusted for letting her thoughts get so out of hand, Jenny whirled away from the mirror and headed for the shower. Her future didn't include a husband and babies. It would be only herself and eventually a twenty-year pin for service well done. Wasn't that what she wanted?

A few minutes later, as Jenny stepped out of the shower, the telephone rang. Knotting the towel between her breasts, she hurried over to the nightstand to answer it.

"Hello."

"Jenny," a man's voice said to her, "this is Joe McCann."

"Oh, hi, Joe," she said to Savanna's husband. "How are you?"

"I'm—well, actually I don't know how I am."

Jenny was suddenly uneasy. "Is anything wrong, Joe? It isn't Savanna, is it?"

He let out a heavy sigh. "I'm afraid it is. That's why I'm calling. She's in the hospital and I thought you'd want to know."

Sweet, dear Savanna in the hospital? Why, the two of them had gone shopping only a few days ago. Savanna had bought a stack of maternity clothes and promised to give them to Jenny once she had the baby. Jenny had told her to quit dreaming, but Savanna had simply laughed that bubbly laugh of hers.

"What's wrong, Joe? Dear God, she hasn't lost the baby, has she?"

"No. Not yet. But the doctors are very concerned. They're afraid the pains she's experiencing are labor pains."

Jenny drew in a sharp breath. "But it's too early! If she goes into labor now—" She couldn't bring herself to finish.

Joe did it for her. "I know, Jenny. At this point, the baby wouldn't survive. But I'm praying that won't happen."

The anguish in Joe's voice ripped right through Jenny. "Of course you are. And I'll be praying, too."

"Thank you for that, Jenny. And I'd like to ask something else of you, if I could?"

"Ask it. Anything," she assured him.

"Well, right now Savanna is pretty scared and the doctor said the last thing she needs is any sort of mental stress. I thought if you came and talked with her, it would bolster her spirits."

"There wasn't any need for you to ask. I'll be there. What hospital is she in?"

He gave her the name. Jenny closed her eyes and sent up a quick little prayer.

"I'll be there in a few minutes," she promised.

After Jenny hung up the phone, she quickly dressed, then headed to the hospital. When she entered Savanna's room, she found her friend white-faced and gripping Joe's hand. Megan was sitting on the edge of her stepmother's bed. It was obvious the teenager was struggling to hold back the tears.

With sudden insight, Jenny knew that if Savanna was to lose this child, she wouldn't be the only one to suffer. Joe and Megan would be shattered too. That was the way of things in a tightly knit family. When one member hurt, so did the rest.

"Megan, now that Jenny is here, why don't you and I go down for a cup of coffee?"

The teenager frowned at her father. "Daddy, I don't drink coffee!"

The three adults smiled. Joe said, "Okay, honey, you can have a cola. And these two women can have a little time to themselves."

"Sure, Daddy." Megan leaned over and kissed Savanna's cheek. "See you in a little bit."

Joe pressed a kiss to Savanna's forehead, then quietly led Megan out of the room.

Once they were gone, Jenny ignored the plastic chair by the bed. Instead she sat on the edge of the mattress and took Savanna's hand in hers.

"What are you doing giving me a scare like this?"

Savanna struggled to smile. "I thought you needed a little excitement in your life."

Jenny made a face at her. "I could do without this kind. How are you feeling?"

A worried frown puckered Savanna's face. "All right, for the moment. At least I'm not having any pains."

Jenny reached up and brushed at Savanna's tousled bangs. "You're going to be fine. You and the baby."

Tears welled up in Savanna's brown eyes. "Oh, Jen," she whispered, "I'm so scared. I want this baby so badly. So does Joe. If I lose it—"

"Hush that sort of talk! You're not going to lose the baby. You're going to do what the doctors tell you to do and you're going to get through this. Do you hear me?"

A wan smile touched Savanna's lips. "Yes, Officer Prescott."

"That's better. I don't want to hear any more negative talk out of you. I want you to lay there and think about how fat you're going to be in a couple of months. Fat and beautiful."

"Oh, Jen, I wish I could be as strong and brave as you are."

To hear Lucas tell it, she had the courage of a field mouse. And looking back on her behavior this past month, she was beginning to agree with him. "Savanna, you're far braver than I ever thought about being."

Savanna knowingly shook her head. "Oh, no. You're the bravest woman I've ever known. And not because of your job. A woman who's been through what you have has to be courageous. So don't try to act humble with me."

Dear Lord, this woman was lying here facing something far more frightening than anything Jenny had ever come up against, and yet she was calling Jenny brave and courageous. It made her feel like a cowardly hypocrite.

"Believe me, Savanna, you have all the courage you need to get through this. So show it to me and give me a smile. A real one. Not one of those sickly little things I saw when I first walked in."

Savanna's lips curved at the corners, then slowly spread into a wide smile. "You're a wonderful friend, Jenny. And you're right. I am going to get through this."

Jenny stayed with Savanna for the rest of the afternoon, then deciding her friend needed rest more than company, she drove to her apartment. On the way, Jenny noticed Christmas decorations were going up in yards and windows. It made her wonder if Savanna would still be safely carrying her child when the holiday arrived. Dear Lord, she hoped so.

And Lucas, what would he be doing on Christmas day? Spending it in Florida with his father, she supposed.

You'd like that trip, Jenny.

Lucas's voice whispered through her mind like the call of a lonesome dove, and her heart began to weep for Savanna and Joe and what they might lose. It cried, too, for herself and Lucas and things that could never be.

You're the bravest woman I know.

This time it was Savanna's words that taunted her as she parked the car, then let her forehead fall wearily against the steering wheel. *I'm not brave,* Jenny silently cried. It was wrong for anyone to think she was! If she had any courage at all, she would have never pushed Lucas out of her life. She would have put her hand in his and held on for all she was worth.

That's just the trouble. You're not worth anything.

Jenny's face went white as she lifted her head and looked all around her. That wasn't herself talking. That was Marcus!

Six years ago Jenny was sure she'd gotten free of him. But now she knew she'd only rid herself of his physical presence, his fist and his vicious mouth. But his memory had hung around to haunt and intimidate her. Only now, at this very moment, did Jenny realize that Marcus was still having his way with her, still controlling her life. Wouldn't he be thrilled to know that, she thought with disgust.

Well, no more! She was stronger and braver than that. Savanna believed it of her. So had Lucas, once. Jenny had to believe it, too.

Marcus was in prison now. He could no longer harm her. And even if he was released, she wouldn't run scared. She'd survived the torture he'd put her through. She could survive anything. She could see that clearly now. But if Lucas hadn't come into her life and shown her what true love was really all about, she might not have ever realized any of this about herself. She might have gone on letting the past darken her future.

Climbing out of the car, she hurried into her apartment and snatched up the phone book. She had to call Lucas. If he never wanted to see her again, she would understand that she was too late. But she had to at least tell him how wrong she'd been.

Her hands shaking, she punched out his home number and waited for the sound of his voice. To her disappointment, it came over an answering machine. Ignoring the invitation to leave a message, she hung up the phone and dialed the offices of L.L. Freight.

"Mr. Lowrimore won't be back in his office until Monday," a woman on the other end told her.

This was only Friday. She couldn't wait that long! "Do you know where I might contact him?"

"I'm afraid not. His secretary might be able to tell you. But she's already gone home for the day."

Jenny thanked the woman and hung up. Lilah would know where to find him.

Jenny crossed her fingers that the woman wasn't out shopping.

"Lilah here," the older woman said cheerfully.

"Lilah, this is Jenny Prescott."

There was a pregnant pause, then she said, "It's good to hear from you, Jenny. How are you doing?"

"Fine now," she said with firm resolution. "The reason I'm calling is Lucas. Do you know where I can find him? Is he out of town?"

Lilah let out a huge sigh of relief. "Oh, thank heavens! You're really going to see Lucas?"

"Yes. I—oh, Lilah, I've been a hundred kinds of fools. Do you think there's any chance he might still want to see me?"

"Jenny, I don't know what went on between you two, but whatever it was has had Lucas behaving strangely. I truly thought that by now he would have already tried to contact you."

"I told him not to."

"Yes, but Lucas never has been one to abide by the rules."

In spite of everything, Jenny's heart began to beat with hope. "Do you think he might still care for me?"

"Oh, my dear, I know he does. Now go to him. He's out at his farmhouse and intends to stay there until Sunday evening."

"I'm on my way!"

Chapter Eleven

Jenny had forgotten how long the drive was to Lucas's house in the country. Or maybe her anxiousness to get there made it seem more like fifty miles rather than twenty-five before she finally reached the drive to the old homestead.

She found Lucas's black truck parked next to the giant sycamore she remembered from her earlier visit. Jenny parked beside the pickup, then walked slowly up the steps and across the long porch.

A power saw was buzzing loudly in a nearby room. Jenny waited until it quieted, then knocked. A moment later, footsteps grew closer and then Lucas was standing in front of her. Sawdust covered his old jeans and navy blue sweatshirt, and his beard looked as though he'd forgotten to shave for several days, but to Jenny, he'd never looked better.

"Jenny!"

"Hello, Lucas."

Her heart pounding, she waited for him to say something. When he failed to make any sort of reply, she said, "Lilah told me you were here. May I come in?"

He hesitated only for a moment, then stepped to one side and allowed her passage into the house. Jenny was immediately struck by the smell of fresh sawdust, paint and just-brewed coffee. The scents took her back to when Lucas had first brought her to this place. He'd had hopes and plans then, and those plans had included her. Why had she been so afraid to love this man? Now it was probably too late to ever have a future with him, she thought with bitter regret.

At the sound of the door shutting behind her, Jenny turned to face him. He looked at her, his gaze cautious and questioning. He obviously didn't trust her, and the idea made her sick with regret.

"Why are you here?" he finally asked.

She swallowed at the lump that had suddenly lodged in her throat. "I wanted to talk to you."

His dark brows lifted mockingly. "Just like that?"

She nodded. "Just like that."

Lucas let his eyes travel slowly over her flushed cheeks and windblown hair, her red coat and black leather dress boots. She was even more beautiful than he remembered, and just looking at her was like a feast to his starving heart.

"I see you're not wearing your uniform, so apparently you're not here to arrest me."

Her nostrils flared at his sarcasm. "This was my day off. I've spent the afternoon at the hospital."

His eyes narrowed. "Hospital? Why?"

"My friend Savanna is in danger of losing her baby."

He looked properly chagrined. "I'm sorry."

"Yes. I am, too. But I'm hoping with everything inside me that she and the baby will be all right."

"I hope so, too."

The sincerity in his voice was real and touched the deepest part of her. "Thank you, Lucas. That means a lot to me."

He took a step toward her. "Does it really, Jenny?"

Suddenly the sight of him plus the torture she'd put herself through this past week were too much for her. She turned her back to him and covered her face with both hands.

"Jenny?"

She drew in a bracing breath and tried to quell her trembling nerves. "I know—I guess you're wondering what I'm doing here."

Lucas should have gotten satisfaction from the pain he heard in her voice. After all, she'd torn his heart out when she'd ordered him to stay away from her. But exacting revenge on Jenny wasn't what he wanted.

"Frankly, I am. The other morning you said you never wanted to see me again. You were emphatic about it, remember?"

"I remember." Her throat was so tight the words came out in a hoarse whisper. "I said a lot of things that morning. All of them wrong."

Like a golden ray of sunshine peeking through a rain cloud, hope entered Lucas's heart. "You didn't think you were wrong. You were pretty vehement about making your feelings clear to me."

Lucas obviously wasn't going to make this apology easy for her, and Jenny could hardly blame him. She'd hurt him badly and she hated herself for that.

Turning, she bravely met his dark, searching gaze. "I guess you must hate me now."

Hate her? Dear God, he loved her wildly, utterly, and nothing could change that. Still, he wasn't about to stand here and put his heart on the line again. Not until he knew what was going on in that beautiful head of hers.

"I don't hate anyone. Especially you."

She took several steps toward him, then stopped. "Lucas, on the way out here I thought of so many things I wanted to say to you, but now I don't know how to say any of them." Her hands lifted, then fell helplessly back to her sides. "I don't know how to explain what happened to me, because I don't really understand it myself."

Lucas could see her eyes begging him to open his mind and his heart to her. And suddenly he could stand it no longer. He closed the gap between them and gently cupped her face with his hands.

"Jenny." He spoke softly. "I suspect you've spent the biggest part of your life being afraid. Of not having a real mother or father, of Marcus's violence, and then later of being alone. Please don't be afraid of me now."

Something inside Jenny gave way and suddenly her heart wasn't cloaked in darkness anymore. Lucas understood! He must have all along, but she'd been too blinded by the past to see it.

Reaching up, she wrapped her fingers around his forearms and held on tightly. "Oh, Lucas, today when I saw Savanna, I—" A flood of emotions suddenly choked her and it was a moment before she could go on. "She was fighting so valiantly for her unborn child, but do you know that she called me the brave one?"

Jenny shook her head before he could make a reply. "I'd never felt like such a hypocrite. And then on the way home I kept thinking about you and all that I'd lost by pushing you out of my life. And I knew I'd done it because I was afraid. For the past five years I'd tried my best to forget I was a woman. I was content just to be a cop. Then you came along and woke me up. You reminded me that I *am* a woman with a woman's needs. And that scared me to the bone."

Her lips were trembling, her voice quivering. The need to comfort her was too strong to resist. Lucas pulled her tightly against his chest and stroked the crown of her head.

"So what did make you decide to drive out here to see me today?"

The circle of his arms around her, the hard warmth of his chest beneath her cheek were like heaven, a warm loving place Jenny never wanted to leave.

"I heard Marcus's voice," she said flatly.

His brows puckered, he eased her back and looked into her face. "You heard Marcus's voice?"

Her admission had obviously stunned him. Jenny knew it sounded crazy, even a bit paranormal, but she didn't care. It had opened her eyes.

Nodding, she said, "At first I thought he was sitting in the car beside me. And then it dawned on me that he was in my head. And that he'd been there all this time, reminding me how worthless I was as a wife and a lover, telling me that there was no point in trying to have a life with you because I could never make you happy."

"And you believed him?" he asked incredulously. "Even though he's been gone all these years, you were still letting him dictate to you?"

Jenny knew it was hard for him to believe. It would be hard for anyone to fathom, unless they'd been through the same things she'd endured.

"You know, Lucas, all these years, even while I was married to Marcus, I thought I had a mind, a will of my own. I did my best to fight back and defend myself. I did my best to break away and build a life on my own. And I did—to a certain extent. But I guess after a woman has been browbeaten and degraded for so long, it does something to her thinking, not to mention her self-esteem.''

"Captain Morgan told me you were one of the best officers on his force. How could you think of yourself as a failure?''

Jenny shrugged. "Oh, I've always been confident as a cop, because that was the one aspect of my life that Marcus couldn't enter. But as a wife and lover, I felt very inept. So when you proposed marriage, all I could see was my failings.''

Lucas shook his head in wondrous disbelief. "The last thing I figured you needed was to hear your ex-husband talking in your ear. But now—well, all I can say is I'm glad he did.''

With hopeful, tentative fingers, she reached up and touched his face. "Does that mean you'll forgive me for being such a blind fool? Can you still love me, or have I managed to destroy all that you ever felt for me?''

Groaning, he buried his face in the side of her neck. She felt warm and wonderful, and her scent reminded him of a bed of spring rosebuds just waiting to burst into bloom.

"You hurt me, Jenny. I won't deny that. But I never stopped loving you. And if you hadn't come to me soon, I would have found some way to make you see the light. I didn't know how I was going to win you over. But I hadn't given up.''

Jenny clutched him close, wondering how she could be so lucky to have a man like Lucas love her.

"You mean you hadn't written me off?''

His hands began to roam her back, then tunnel into her hair. Tipping her head back, he lowered his lips close to hers. "You really didn't think I could write you off, did you?''

She nodded and he was reminded once again of how little worth she placed on herself. "I was afraid you had already started looking for that strong woman you've always wanted."

Lucas suddenly smiled, and like the wind after the rain, Jenny's doubts blew away and brilliant sunshine poured into her heart.

"Oh, Lucas, I love you. I'm going to spend the rest of my life showing you how much."

Words had ceased to be enough for Lucas. His lips hungrily took hers. His hands crushed her tightly against him. For long moments the kiss spoke for both of them. And they each said, "I love you."

When Lucas finally lifted his head, Jenny let out a breathless laugh. "It feels wonderful to be a woman again."

Lucas's dark eyes glinted sexily. "You feel pretty wonderful to me," he assured her, then his face grew serious and he gently traced a loving circle on her cheek. "I know it took courage for you to come to me like this and open yourself up. Now I've got to be just as brave and tell you that if you still want to be a cop after we marry, then that's what I want you to do. I don't ever want to be guilty of taking anything from you, Jenny. I want to give to you. Everything. Anything you want. And that includes you being a police officer."

She couldn't believe Lucas loved her that much. It was hard for her to imagine that any man would put her wants before his own. But Lucas was special. Maybe that's why she'd been so struck by him that first day she'd met him.

"You'd worry about me," she pointed out. "You'd constantly be afraid you might lose me the same way you lost your friend."

Lucas nodded gravely. "Yes. But I'd learn to deal with it. You've survived ten years on the force. I'm hoping like hell you can make it through the next ten without meeting up with a bullet or a knife blade."

Jenny shook her head at him, then, smiling, she pressed her cheek against his. "Being a cop these past ten years was good for me. At the time it was the right thing for me to do. But not now. These next ten years you'll not see me in a blue uniform. All I want is to be your wife and, I hope, the mother of your children."

Taking her by the shoulders, he looked deep into her eyes. "Are you sure?"

"I've never been more sure about anything in my life!"

The firm resolution in her voice told Lucas he had to believe her. Laughing with pure joy, he lifted Jenny off her feet and kissed her soundly on the lips.

His eyes sparkling down at her, he said, "Jenny, darling, the Ray Lowrimore House is opening its doors a week before Christmas. My father is flying up for the ceremony and then I'd planned to drive him back to Florida and stay there through the holiday. Do you think you might want to spend our Christmas honeymoon on a warm, sandy beach? Or would you rather head to the cold and the snow?"

Rising on tiptoe, she slid her arms around his neck. "I've had enough cold emptiness in my life to last a lifetime. Give me heat. I'll be ready," she told him, then with an impish smile she added, "as soon as I buy a new swimsuit."

His grin was devilish. "A bikini?"

She looked shocked. "I'm too old for one of those, Lucas!"

Laughing under his breath, Lucas said, "You're not too old for anything, darlin', and I'm going to enjoy every second of proving it to you."

He kissed her again, then Jenny glanced regretfully around the room. "I wish you had a phone here. I'd call Savanna and tell her the good news."

"Your wish is my command," he said gladly.

His arm snug around her waist, Lucas guided her to the kitchen. "Since I planned to stay here over the weekend, I brought my cellular phone with me," he explained.

Jenny jerked off her coat, then dived for the instrument on the counter.

"You're sure you don't mind? I mean, calls on these things are outrageous!"

Lucas laughed and picked up the receiver. "Jenny, you're forgetting I'm a man who doesn't have to count his pennies."

"Oh, I forgot," she said, with sudden understanding.

A wry smile on his face, he said, "At least I know you're not marrying me for my money."

"No. My reasons are purely selfish. I love you."

To reward her, he got the hospital on the line, then handed her the receiver. By the time Savanna answered, Jenny was practically bouncing on her toes with excitement.

"Savanna, it's Jenny. How are you feeling?"

"Oh, Jenny, I'm so glad you called! Joe's been trying to get you all evening. We wanted to let you know the results of the test the doctors ran earlier today are back and we got good news."

"Really? Tell me," Jenny urged.

"There's been no harm to the baby and the pains were brought on by a hormonal imbalance."

"Isn't that bad?"

"Not when it's something that can easily be taken care of with medication. The doctor said now that he knows what the problem is, he can safely treat it and I should expect to deliver a healthy baby boy in four months."

Relief and joy flooded through Jenny. Glancing at Lucas, she silently mouthed that Savanna was going to be all right.

"Thank God, Savanna. I'm so happy for all of you." Jenny smiled at Lucas and he gave her a happy wink. "So do you think you can stand some more good news?"

"Good news? What is it? You're being promoted?"

Jenny laughed. "You might say that."

"Jen, you're actually laughing. And your voice, it just doesn't sound like you at all. What's going on?"

"Do you think that little boy of yours would appreciate having a new cousin to play with?"

Clearly confused, Savanna answered, "I'm sure he would. But since Joe and I have no brothers or sisters, I don't see that happening."

"Well, just give me and Lucas a few months and it will happen."

"Jenny! Are you saying—are you and Lucas going to get married after all?"

Like a bubbling fountain, Jenny quickly went on to tell Savanna the plans that she and Lucas had made so far. By the time Jenny hung up the phone both women were crying tears of joy.

Lucas wiped Jenny's face and led her into the dining room and over to the large bay window. "Do you remember when I asked you about building a window seat here?"

Jenny nodded with fond remembrance. "I told you I'd never had a house with a window seat. I told you I'd never even had a house!"

The sound of her happy laughter filled him up, and he knew with Jenny in his life, he'd never feel empty again. Hugging her close, he said, "Well, now we're going to sit here together, drink our coffee and watch our children play in the yard."

For long moments they both stood looking out the window and simply marveling at the idea of being together for the rest of their lives.

"You know," Lucas said after a while, "I've got to hire a crew of carpenters out here to get this place ready for us to move into. Spring will be here before we know it and I want us to be living here when the redbud begins to blossom." He glanced at her as something else struck him. "Jenny, about the barn I'm turning into a shelter."

She looked at him eagerly. "Yes?"

"There will be a hired staff to run it and care for the children. But if you think it's too close, if you're afraid the shelter will invade our lives, I'll find another place to build it."

Jenny swiftly shook her head. "No! I'd never want you to do that. Your generosity and concern for those kids are part of the reason I love you. In fact," she went on, her expression growing thoughtful, "you probably know yourself that a lot of those children you help have abused mothers. If there was room for, say, two or three women to stay in the shelter, too, I would love to have the chance to help those women. What do you think?"

At that moment, Lucas couldn't have been more proud of her.

Drawing her gently into his arms, he said, "I think I was right about you that very first day you walked up and ordered me to get out of my car. You're a hell of a woman, Jenny."

Her eyes softly inviting, she reached up and tugged his head down to hers. "And you're one good man, Lucas Lowrimore."

*   *   *   *   *

COMING NEXT MONTH

#1144 MOST WANTED DAD—Arlene James
Fabulous Fathers/This Side of Heaven
Amy Slater knew the teenage girl next door needed a sympathetic ear—as did her father, Evans Kincaid. But Amy found it hard to be just a *friend* to the sexy lawman, even though she'd sworn never to love again....

#1145 DO YOU TAKE THIS CHILD?—Marie Ferrarella
The Baby of the Month Club
One night of passion with handsome Slade Garret left Dr. Sheila Pollack expecting nothing...except a baby! When Slade returned and demanded marriage, Sheila tried to resist. But Slade caught her at a weak moment—while she was in labor!

#1146 REILLY'S BRIDE—Patricia Thayer
Women were in demand in Lost Hope, Wyoming, so why did Jenny Murdock want stubborn rancher Luke Reilly, the only man *not* looking for a wife? Now Jenny had to convince Reilly he needed a bride....

#1147 MOM IN THE MAKING—Carla Cassidy
The Baker Brood
Bonnie Baker was in Casey's Corners to hide from love, not to be swept away by town catch Russ Blackburn! Gorgeous, devilish Russ got under her skin all right...but could Bonnie ever risk love again?

#1148 HER VERY OWN HUSBAND—Lauryn Chandler
Rose Honeycutt had just blown out her birthday candles when a handsome drifter showed up on her doorstep. Cowboy Skye Hanks was everything she'd wished for, but would his mysterious past keep them from a future together?

#1149 WRANGLER'S WEDDING—Robin Nicholas
Rachel Callahan would do anything to keep custody of her daughter. So when Shane Purcell proposed a pretend engagement, Rachel decided to play along. Little did she know that the sexy rodeo rogue was playing for keeps!

MILLION DOLLAR SWEEPSTAKES

It's time you joined...

THE BABY OF THE MONTH CLUB

Silhouette Desire proudly presents *Husband: Optional*, book four of RITA Award-winning author Marie Ferrarella's miniseries, THE BABY OF THE MONTH CLUB, coming your way in March 1996.

She wasn't fooling him. Jackson Cain knew the baby Mallory Flannigan had borne was his...no matter that she *claimed* a conveniently absentee lover was Joshua's true dad. And though Jackson had left her once to "find" his true feelings, nothing was going to keep him away from this ready-made family now....

Do You Take This Child? We certainly hope you do, because in April 1996 Silhouette Romance will feature this final book in Marie Ferrarella's wonderful miniseries, THE BABY OF THE MONTH CLUB, found only in— *Silhouette*®

As seen on TV!
Free Gift Offer

With a Free Gift proof-of-purchase from any Silhouette® book,
you can receive a beautiful cubic zirconia pendant.

This gorgeous marquise-shaped stone is a genuine cubic
zirconia—accented by an 18" gold tone necklace.

(Approximate retail value $19.95)

Send for yours today...
compliments of ▼ *Silhouette®*

TM

To receive your free gift, a cubic zirconia pendant, send us one original proof-of-
purchase, photocopies not accepted, from the back of any Silhouette Romance™,
Silhouette Desire®, Silhouette Special Edition®, Silhouette Intimate Moments®
or Silhouette Shadows™ title available in February, March or April at your favorite
retail outlet, together with the Free Gift Certificate, plus a check or money order for
$1.75 U.S./$2.25 CAN. (do not send cash) to cover postage and handling, payable
to Silhouette Free Gift Offer. We will send you the specified gift. Allow 6 to 8 weeks for
delivery. Offer good until April 30, 1996 or while quantities last. Offer valid in the U.S. and
Canada only.

Free Gift Certificate

Name: _____

Address: _____

City: _____ State/Province: _____ Zip/Postal Code: _____

Mail this certificate, one proof-of-purchase and a check or money order for postage
and handling to: SILHOUETTE FREE GIFT OFFER 1996. In the U.S.: 3010 Walden
Avenue, P.O. Box 9057, Buffalo NY 14269-9057. In Canada: P.O. Box 622, Fort Erie,

---

FREE GIFT OFFER   079-KBZ-R

ONE PROOF-OF-PURCHASE

To collect your fabulous FREE GIFT, a cubic zirconia pendant, you must include this
original proof-of-purchase for each gift with the properly completed Free Gift Certificate.

079-KBZ-R

MOM IN THE MAKING
by Carla Cassidy

Book two of her miniseries

"I don't need a mommy, but Miss Bonnie *would* be perfect. Now, if I can just convince daddy…"
—Daniel Blackburn, age 8

"Little Daniel is so sweet. All he needs is a little TLC, and his hunk of a dad could use some loving, too!"
—Bonnie Baker, mom in the making

"My son adores Bonnie, but this sexy lady just isn't mother material—is she?"
—Russ Blackburn, single dad

Look for *Mom in the Making* in April.

The Baker Brood miniseries continues for two more months:
An Impromptu Proposal in May, and
Daddy on the Run in June…only from

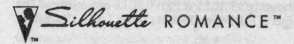

Silhouette ROMANCE™

You're About to Become a  *Privileged Woman*

Reap the rewards of fabulous free gifts and benefits with proofs-of-purchase from Silhouette and Harlequin books

Pages & Privileges™

It's our way of thanking you for buying our books at your favorite retail stores.

Harlequin and Silhouette— the most privileged readers in the world!

For more information about Harlequin and Silhouette's PAGES & PRIVILEGES program call the Pages & Privileges Benefits Desk: 1-503-794-2499

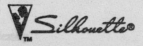

Silhouette®